THE EXTRAORDINARY ADVENTURES

OF

MAX MALONE

VOLUME II AMERICAN EXPLORERS

DAN VANDERBURG

TO: Callie

Best Wishes

Dan Vanderburg

ISBN: 9781690620198

Acknowledgements

Thanks go out again to my daughter, Tina Vanderburg for making Max come to life with her creative cover design and internal formatting. This book would never have seen the light of day without her technical wizardry. Thanks, Tina for all you do.

I also want to thank the members of The Granbury Writers' Bloc for their input and encouragement helping me to become better at what I do.

THE EXTRAORDINARY ADVENTURES of MAX MALONE

VOLUME II

AMERICAN EXPLORERS

PROLOGUE

So, what's up this summer? Oh, just the regular stuff like riding my bike. I'll probably pull some skateboard stunts and hang out with the guys a lot. I might even gather enough courage to try Rick's new elevated skateboard ramps that he and his dad built in his backyard. I'm sure I'll play a little vacant lot baseball with the guys. We'll probably go swimming some at the city park pool, and I'll ask the guys to come over to work out with the round ball on our driveway. So, I'm just an average fourteen-year-old-kid doing regular, everyday kid stuff.

And oh, by the way—I'm also a shape-shifting, body jumping, time traveler!

What? Yeah, it's true! I can travel in time. If it sounds exciting—it is! With help from Doctor Magas, I can go anywhere in the past and jump into the body of anyone I want, at any time in their life.

Sounds ridiculous and impossible? I thought so too—for a while. I thought that I was just having wild and crazy, but very vivid dreams. That is until I learned I was actually time traveling.

Not just anybody can time travel, right? *Nobody* can except me and Doctor Magas. He can do it because of his special magical powers. I have those powers too. How this all came down for me is a really bizarre story, so let me back up and start from the beginning. This whole thing is just too weird to not explain thoroughly.

You see, a couple of months ago, I had an assignment in history class to write a research report about early Texas. All Texas kids study Texas history in the seventh grade. So, I went to the school library to find a book to use for the research. As I walked between the rows, the strangest thing happened.

This big, old book essentially took control of my hands and arms, causing me to take it off the top shelf and check it out to take home. You would think that something that spooky would freak me out, but it didn't. It all felt very natural. Believe it or not, I had no clue even what the book was about or its title. Isn't that nuts? Somehow, I just knew it was the right book for me.

That's when I met Doctor Magas. He was the substitute school librarian. He was taking the place of the regular librarian who was on leave to have a baby. At first, I thought he was just a peculiar old guy with a bit of a European accent.

Boy, was I wrong! I soon learned that he's a very special person. He's a well-educated scientist, historian, and archaeologist with two Ph.D. degrees. He's studied, researched and written about the history of all civilizations. He's also directed scientific archeological digs all over the world.

Oh yeah—he's also a magician. No, not the kind of magician that does card tricks or stunts like sawing women in half to entertain people on TV or at the circus. He's a real magician from a line of many generations of ancestors with very special and strong powers. It's in his DNA. He's worked his entire life to develop, strengthen and combine those powers with sophisticated and advanced science to develop the ability to safely travel back and forth into the past. He's done it hundreds of times. Now he's teaching me!

He also, as I've just recently learned, is my grandfather! Woah! What a surprise.

As it turns out, he and my grandmother, in eastern Europe as teenagers, were in love and wanted to marry, but her father prohibited it because the young man was a gypsy. His family had a terrible reputation. Along with palm reading and fortune telling, they were also considered scoundrels and thieves by the local population.

After my grandmother refused to stop seeing her young man when her father forbade it, her father shipped her and his wife to America. It took her father a while to sell his home and business in Europe and immigrate himself. He joined his family in America almost a year later. What a surprise he had when his daughter presented him with his new granddaughter. That was my mom.

My grandfather broke away from his family and their dishonest ways and pursued a life of study of the natural sciences and history and searching for his missing love. He never knew of his daughter and her family until just recently.

Grandpa's investigation into the past brought him to our town last year. He was directing an archeological dig close by, looking for pre-Clovis artifacts when he received a clue that my grandmother and her family were here. Unfortunately, he was too late to reunite with her. She died the year before.

He didn't know how to grieve a love he'd lost so many years earlier, but he hoped he could find and be united with the daughter he'd never known, and his grandchildren.

He retired from his daily work of researching history and archeology, found and bought a fine, old, historic home in our town and rebuilt it to suit his needs. He ultimately found my family just recently through meeting me at school. We're all still getting to know each other. Of course, I know him better than the others so far, and I'm really excited about how he's changed my life.

Now to explain the time travel thing. Doctor Magas puts his magic in a very special bookmarker. When I place the marker in the spine of the book I'm reading about historical events, I'm all of a sudden transported back to that time and place. I've done a bunch of trips so far, exploring Texas history for my school assignment. Oh, I aced the report for that history assignment too.

So, it's the last day of school and I'm back at the library looking for more adventures.

CHAPTER 1

"**What wild adventures** do you have for me next?" I wore an eager smile as I stepped up to the school library counter. My arms were wrapped around the book I needed to return. Doctor Magas worked behind the counter checking books in that kids returned before the summer vacation started.

"Hi Max," he said as he took a break from scanning the digital reader across the book's barcodes. "Didn't know if I'd see you today or not, with it being such a busy day—last day of school and all.

"I see you're returning it." His eyes softened and the whiskers of his neatly trimmed, white beard framed a smile.

"You want more adventure? You mean you didn't get your fill with that book? Quite a series of stories, wasn't it?"

"Boy, I'll say! I hope the next book is as good."

He reached underneath the counter and drew out a big, leather-covered book. He clutched it to his chest for a moment, almost caressing it before putting it carefully on the counter. It looked much like the one I was returning.

"Now that I know how much you like adventure, I'm sure you'll enjoy this one, and you'll learn so much," he said resting his hand on the book. It's loaded with exploration and excitement."

"What kind of exploration?"

"It's about daring people that sought adventure discovering America. It's about the explorers, trailblazers, and pioneers looking for a better way of life. It introduces you to ordinary people that find themselves caught up in extraordinary circumstances." He raised his eyebrows, tilted his head and looked at me over the thin, gold rims of his glasses in that knowing expression of his. "I think you'll like it."

"I know I will if it's like the last one."

"Where's the bookmark?" he asked. A small worry line started to form between his eyes.

"Oh, I have it right here." I reached into my jeans pocket and pulled out the leather marker. It was about two inches wide and five inches long. I'd folded it in two. It was a soft, old looking piece of leather with several strange markings on it that looked like they'd been branded or burned into the leather. I handed it to him.

"You must remember, Max; this is your key to adventure. Take very good care of it." He opened the book to a page in the front, gently placed the bookmark in the spine and closed the cover. "Now, go—enjoy—explore."

I met Rick and Jeremy at the lockers for the walk home. Rick was cleaning out his locker. Notes had been posted on the lockers two weeks earlier stating that they must be emptied before the summer break. Jeremy and I had cleaned ours out last week, but, of course, Rick waited until the last minute to do his. I stood back and watched Jeremy hold a black trash bag open while Rick tossed stuff into it from his locker. In a pile at his feet to take home were two winter coats, a hoodie, an extra pair of old sneakers, and a soccer ball.

"Oh, my gosh!" Jeremy said. He recoiled from the trash bag as Rick tossed a stained, lunch-sized paper bag inside. "What do you have in there?"

"Best I can tell, it's several science experiments gone bad." Rick peeked into another small bag, then quickly closed and tossed it. "From the looks of the green and black fuzzy stuff growing inside, I guess I forgot some snacks Mom sent to school with me several weeks—or months ago. Looks like some pretty toxic stuff." He quickly tossed it into the garbage bag as he made a face and turned his head away from the stink. "Huh, I been wondering what that funny smell was."

"Funny smell?" Jeremy croaked. "That's a five-alarm, puke on your shoes stink! Come on, get that stuff outta there so I can close the trash bag."

"Aw, quit your bellyaching," Rick said. "You know you want a bite." He shook another open sack in Jeremy's face.

Jeremy dropped the trash bag and jumped away. "Hey, Dude, what's wrong with you? You can finish that disaster you call a locker by yourself." He noticed me standing a few feet away. "Hey Max, you got a gas mask in your backpack?"

"No, I'm fresh out, sorry. Come on Rick, finish that up. We've got summer vacation waiting for us."

While we waited for Rick to finish, I put the big book in my backpack. That's when I noticed the warm, special feeling of the book for the first time. While I handled it, it glowed, not a light-emitting glow, but a special feeling glow, sorta like a tiny vibration. I wasn't surprised. It was like the other book I returned to Doctor

Magas. It was a nice, comforting feel, kinda like I had a good trusted friend in my backpack.

Rick finally finished with his locker, sealed and tossed the plastic bag in a trash can outside the building and we turned our backs on school for the summer. The walk home was quieter than normal. Rick, usually the instigator of weird conversation, was busy keeping up with the gear he was returning home along with his fully loaded backpack. We were also planning our summer activities.

We decided not to make a specific schedule for baseball or basketball practice but would just give each other a call a couple of days a week or stop by to get together. Last summer, we spent lots of time hanging out; working on our skateboard moves or exploring the town on our bikes. I'd known both those guys for years, and we lived within a couple of blocks of each other, so we'd have plenty of time together over the summer.

But I had other important things on my mind. This would be my first summer to have all the time I want to explore the past. I'm still getting used to the outrageous fact that I'm now a real-live time traveler and can body jump into whoever I want, anytime in the past to live their adventures with them. This discovery has shaken me, but has offered a whole new world of discovery that I could never have dreamed of before.

I found Mom home when I came in and stashed my backpack by the stairs.

"Hey," she called from the kitchen. She was sitting on a stool at the island counter sorting a packet of grocery coupons.

"How was your last day at school?"

I sat on a stool next to her. "Not much goin' on. All of us, including the teachers, were ready to be outta there."

"You know, I was just thinking about you when you walked in. Your dad and I were talking about you and Megan last night. You know we're really proud of you. You're so helpful around the house, and your kid's chef nights are such a help to me. You know, you've really become a good cook."

I grinned. "You know I enjoy it."

"It shows. Your dad also appreciates the help you give him around here too with the weekend outdoor projects. We're really happy with what you've done with your grades this year too. No C's this last time. All A's and B's. Mostly A's. I don't know what's going on, but it seems like you're more focused now. I guess you're just growing up."

"Thanks, Mom. I *did* enjoy school more this year. None of the subjects gave me much trouble. I even managed to keep up and understand the math. But I really got into history, especially during the last couple of months since I met Doctor Magas. He's helped me a lot."

"You know he *is* your grandfather. It would probably be okay with him if you called him something other than Doctor Magas away from school."

"I know. But I've never had a grandfather before. We've only known him such a short while. I've thought about it. I don't know... Maybe I could call him Grampa. What do you think?"

"I think that's something you may want to talk to him about. It will work if you're both comfortable with it. You'll figure it out."

I changed the subject. "So, what's for dinner?"

"Well, since you and Megan have both done so well this school year, I thought we should have a steak dinner tonight to celebrate. I bought some nice steaks this afternoon."

"Great! Can I grill?"

"Yes, you *may*."

"I mean, *may* I grill?"

"Thank you," she grinned. "I'd love the help."

The dinner was a good family celebration. The steaks were thick and tender. I grilled vegetables and potatoes with the steaks, adding spices and lime juice as they cooked. After Megan got home, she made a fresh garden salad and whipped up a custard for dessert.

Megan and I had been doing kid's chef night for the family once a week for two years under Mom's direction, so we had become pretty good cooks.

When Dad got home, he repeated much of what Mom told me earlier and congratulated Megan on how well she's juggling an active social life with her friends, her Saturday job at the florist, and keeping her straight-A average at school.

I was beginning to get antsy during dessert. Seemed like conversation dragged on with Megan going into detail about a prank she and her friends pulled on one of the girl's boyfriend. I wanted to get into my next adventure.

CHAPTER 2

Anxious to start Grampa's book, I headed to my room after dinner and cleanup. I picked it up and read through the table of contents, looking at the chapter titles. Grampa was right. It was loaded with stories about the discovery and exploration of America. It covered adventures from the cavemen to the opening of the west. I decided to learn from the very beginning.

I hurried through my bedtime routine and slid between the sheets on my belly. After opening the book to the chapter detailing the very first American explorers, I positioned the special book marker in the book's spine and started reading.

The First Americans

Tens of thousands of years ago human beings crossed a land bridge from Asia to North America during the waning period of the Ice Age. They were following the large animals of that time for food.

The descendants of those resilient stone-age explorers followed their food sources and explored their new home. Over thousands of years, they populated all of North America to the Atlantic Ocean and to the southern tip of South America.

I was suddenly startled, but not surprised. A minuscule flash of sparkles erupted from the bookmarker in the spine of the book and tiny particles, kind of like what I would imagine to be fairy dust, settled over me. I knew what to expect but didn't know exactly when it would happen. My now familiar and comfortable trip back in time had started. It was almost like watching a freaky sci-fi movie when my aura lifted from my sleeping body and drifted overhead. I floated like a vapor away from my room and my house.

Now a veteran time traveler, I consider the journey back and forth just part of the process—a very pleasant part. The first few times, though, I didn't know what to make of it. I thought the whole thing was just a vivid dream. But I soon learned I had really become a part of another time.

My spirit transported through time at an unimaginable speed. Images flashed before me—flickering scenes from the past. The first few images were modern-day scenes. Then they started regressing deeper into the past. I saw pioneer people. Then the times before white people—just Indians. Strange animals appeared. Wooly mammoths were there, along with weird looking camels and small horse-like creatures. Some were fierce like huge wolves and saber-toothed tigers.

The last scenes I saw must have been from the Ice Age. Ice and snow covered everything. The backward moving scenes slowed and came to a stop. If I hadn't experienced it all before, I'd be totally bewildered by what came next.

I morphed into another person—a different person from me. My spirit jumped into the body of someone in a totally different time—thousands of years ago.

I knew when, where and who I was. I was a young man, hunting with my clan members, trying to bring meat home to feed our families. I had seen sixteen winters and was one of the younger men on the hunt, but we had two boys with us that hadn't seen their tenth winter. My woman and baby son were waiting for us with the other women and children at the cave. The only food we were able to provide for the clan the last few days was only a few fish from where we'd chopped holes in the ice. Even the fishing failed us because of the thick ice now coating the river.

I gasped for air as I pushed through the snow. *How much longer can I run?* We'd been hunting all day. Three other men ran with me. We'd separated a female wooly mammoth from her small herd out on the prairie and had driven her into the woods. We were trying to force her against a canyon wall. The rest of the men in the clan worked to funnel her toward us. She'd broken away from us once already. We wouldn't have the strength to chase her down if she escaped again. Nobody on the hunt had eaten today. Most of us only had a few bites of food yesterday.

There were twelve of us on the hunt. Three old men stayed back in the cave with the women and children. We all knew they couldn't keep up with us. One was crippled, and the other two were too sick to travel.

The only food the women had to feed the hungry children was their milk. Some of the women's milk was drying up because they hadn't had enough to eat. We *had* to kill this beast to save our clan from starvation.

My companions and I took up hiding places by the canyon wall. I found a vertical crevice in the rock that concealed me. The other three found places to hide behind boulders and trees.

I leaned against the wall, shaking my head and blinking my eyes, trying to will the light-headedness away. My fingers trembled uncontrollably. I consciously slowed my breathing with deep breaths as I waited for the beast to show herself. *I must have food soon.*

I ran my tongue over my dry lips, trying to moisten them. They were cracked from the cold, dry air. Sweat trickled down my chest from running. If I didn't let my body dry, the moisture would freeze. I loosened the ties on my fur jumper to allow air inside and pulled my hood aside as I waited. The sting of the icy wind on my damp head helped clear my mind.

I checked my wooden spear point to make sure I hadn't damaged it during the run. I'd spent part of the day before chipping at the tip to sharpen it. Then I hardened it in the fire. I hoped it was sharp enough. Men had died in hunts like this because their weapons failed.

I also carried a wooden club with a heavy, round rock tied to a fork at the end. Sometimes the club is used to finish off an animal after it's taken down. It would be useless on such a large animal as the mammoth. A sharp spear is the only way to finish off one of them.

We don't throw our spears at animals as large as the wooly mammoth. Their hides are too thick and tough. We must penetrate the skin by forcefully hand-thrusting the spear into a critical area like the throat or belly with as much force as possible to get it to penetrate. It takes a number of men tormenting the beast with their spears after it's tired from a long run to take it down.

I heard men yelling in the distance. They were making as much noise as possible, driving the beast toward us.

The four of us remained hidden and quiet until the beast burst into the clearing only a few yards from us. We showed ourselves, waved our arms and yelled, stopping her forward movement as the rest of the men closed in. We had her surrounded and against the wall. She tried to bolt away toward a man; trying to run him down.

"Now!" I yelled, and several men closest to her closed the gap and thrust their spears. One lodged in her shoulder, doing little harm, but enraging her more. We had her backed against a rock canyon wall with no place to go except through twelve men. We weren't going to let that happen. She slung her head back and forth, trumpeting in her fear and rage, attacking with her long, curved tusks. She stepped to her left, breathing hard, flinging her head and tusks toward me with all the weight of her body behind the motion. I managed to sidestep enough for the left tusk to swing past me as she tore her head upward, trying to impale me. She swung her head back the other way, going after a man attempting to get close enough to make a spear attack. Doing so, she turned her huge head completely away from me, exposing her neck and chest. That's when I lunged.

"Haah!" I screamed drawing back and plunging the spear. My feet left the ground as I drove my spear hard as I could with my forward motion, pushing it with all my weight through her thick skin, into her neck, and deep into her chest. She went to one knee, stayed there for a few seconds, then fell to her side. Several more well-placed spear thrusts finished her off.

We were too exhausted and out of breath to celebrate. Some men fell to their knees to catch their breath and recover from the long run and final fight. Others, like myself, leaned against or sat on the beast to recover.

We couldn't rest long. We were too hungry to let that huge pile of meat just lie there. We tore into it. Each of us carried a thin stone about the size of our hand that we had chipped away one side, creating a cutting edge.

Since I made the killing thrust, it was my honor to claim the choice internal organs to eat raw, on the spot. I wasted no time getting to the heart. I hacked away with the other men, digging our cutting tools over and over across the tough hide, finally cutting through. We worked quickly and quietly. Our hunger drove us.

I thrust my hands inside the animal's body, letting the warmth of the internal organs seep into my near-frozen fingers. I closed my eyes and took a moment to enjoy the rare warmth. Steam from the beast's insides meeting the cold air wafted over my face. I expertly pushed organs aside and reached under the massive rib cage to find the heart.

Working by feel and memory in the warm body, I cut the blood vessels loose and pulled the huge heart from the body.

"Yahee," I hooted as I held the heart high in the air for all to see before I thrust it into my mouth. I bit off all I could chew and passed it around to share the thrill of the kill with my mates.

16

Almost immediately, I could feel strength returning as the rich meat went into my body.

Another man freed the large liver. It was also passed around for everyone to help regain their strength. We worked the rest of the afternoon butchering the beast and separating the meat into pieces small enough to carry back to our cave. We were losing daylight as we finished collecting as much as we could carry.

A pack of wolves assembled not far from where we worked. I'd heard their howling and calls most of the afternoon. The smell of our kill carried long distances on the wind and attracted hungry scavengers. Vultures circled overhead and occasionally took to the ground to watch from a few feet away; impatiently waiting their chance. The wolves were more aggressive than the big birds. They wanted our trophy and they weren't waiting for it.

I sighted the wolves as they came through the woods toward us while we hurried to load our bounty into skin bags and onto our shoulders. They'd held back all they were going to. They were making their move on us. I counted at least ten of them coming through the trees. They weren't charging. Not yet anyway. They slowly moved our way; heads down and tails tightly tucked under their bellies, driven by hunger, ready to burst into action. Their piercing eyes watched our every move. Their lips lifted, exposing their sharp, yellow teeth as they gave off their angry, low-throated growls. Their hackles raised, signaling their intent to attack. They were more hungry than afraid of us. They were fighters and killers. Mere men couldn't stand between them and life-sustaining food for long.

It was past time for us to go. Plenty of meat was still on the mammoth's carcass; more than we could carry, and a bounty for them.

"Go," Baht said, nodding toward the trail in the snow we'd made earlier along the base of the cliff wall. Baht was the head man of our clan. We were all ready to move out with the heavy loads on our backs, bending us over.

As soon as we left the bloody pile of tusks, hair, skin, bones, guts, and an enormous amount of meat that we couldn't carry, the wolves moved in. The vultures that sunk their claws on the carcass as soon as we left scattered but didn't go far. There would still be a meal for them when the wolves finished.

I watched over my shoulder as the wolves tore into the remains of the mammoth, establishing their pecking order. The dominant males took their position of authority over the lesser members of their pack, growling and snapping, sometimes attacking, pushing them aside. I was glad they were satisfied to take the dead animal on the ground rather than the live men moving away.

We were not out of danger. We were far from the safety of our cave. The sun was setting. We had to push on through the darkness until we got our trophy home. Although we were on the move, we were a target for the always hungry wild animals. The darkness was filled with animals—bears, cats, wolves and others on the verge of starvation. We would be more of a target if we stopped for the night to cook meat to eat over a fire. The aroma and smoke of cooking meat in the open would attract scavengers for miles. We couldn't stop to rest. We shouldered our loads and trudged on.

Hours later we reached the river and our cave. It was on the wall of a steep cliff, high above the water. It was a difficult climb, but a safe place, and was sheltered from wind and weather.

"We have food," I shouted as we approached the cave entrance, awakening the clan. Soon the women brought the fires to life and had meat cooking over the flames. The entire clan; men, women, children, and the few old people gathered around the fires to enjoy a rare midnight feast.

While I ate my fill and watched the others do the same, I thought about the ongoing problem with the clan. It was a constant battle that we were losing to keep a clan this size fed. Although this meat would last several days, I was already worried about where we would get our next food.

Basket fishing in the river that the women do when they can punch a hole in the ice is unreliable. Our men are all skilled hunters, but we frequently come back empty-handed, which means empty stomachs for our clan. The weather is so harsh, it makes everything we do difficult. There is little opportunity to gather edibles that the animals haven't already taken with so much ice and snow covering the ground. We all have difficulty with the slick ice on the canyon wall as we try to go back and forth to the cave. The babies and small children are so fragile. Sometimes their little bodies just can't tolerate the cold, no matter how careful we try to protect them.

My woman and I have known for some time that we must do something different so our family can survive and thrive. Our clan has grown in size over the years to the point that it is now too big to sustain itself. It takes a big kill every few days to keep us all fed. We've lost several babies due to the harsh conditions and lack of enough food.

That night lying under the furs on our bed of straw, my woman, Aung, turned to me, "I think we should go," she said. "I've talked to Tuk and Nep, and they agreed. Have you spoken to their men?"

"Yes," I said. We talked about it after the travelers came two moons ago, and again in the last few days. We agree that it is what we must do."

Three moons earlier, two young travelers came to our cave and spent some days with our clan visiting and telling us of their homeland. They came to find wives. All the women and girls in their clan were sisters and cousins. They could not be wives to those young men.

"Our home is different than here," one of the men said. "It is much warmer, with less snow and ice. We have open prairies as far as you can see with lots of grass for many animals to feed."

The other man talked of lands farther away than theirs. "Far away, many moons walking, travelers tell of land with no ice, no snow. So much fish and animals, nobody ever goes hungry. Women pick fruit, nuts, and berries much of the year."

When they left, they took two young women from our clan with them back to their home, far to the south. Our clan elders knew that our clan was already too big and agreed that the young women should go with those men back to their home. One of the women was my young sister. She had seen fourteen winters and was ready for a man. The other was my cousin that had seen thirteen winters. The young men gave our elders two wolverine furs to buy the young women.

I had been talking to my friends, young men my age, and my woman had been talking to their women about leaving our overcrowded clan and traveling south to find warmer weather and better hunting and fishing. We would establish our own clan there, and we would be the elders. The time was right to go. All of us were healthy, including the children.

The next morning, I gathered my two friends outside the cave. We sat in the sun and talked.

"We should act on our plan," I said. "I told my woman we should not delay. We should go now. The clan has enough food for a few days and there is enough for us to take our share. The clan has hunters to survive without us. Are you both ready to do this?" They looked at each other and back at me. We smiled and nodded in agreement as we clasped hands to seal the agreement. We went back to the cave, broke our news to the elders and the rest of the clan while our women packed our few belongings.

Soon we were ready to leave the place that had been our home for the last five winters. After hugs and tears were shared, we gathered our women, children, and belongings and left the cave. We climbed to the top of the canyon wall to the flatlands and headed south to a new life in a new land, leaving our tracks in the snow behind us.

I felt the changes coming over me. I saw the flash of sparkling light as I left the body of the early man leading his new clan into the unknown. As usual, my transformation was comfortable and calming. I enjoyed seeing the flashes of images moving forward in time. Hundreds of them presented themselves to me as my aura sped through the ages.

CHAPTER 3

I slept in that morning, a Saturday, enjoying the first day of summer vacation. When I awoke, I stayed in bed for several minutes, stretching and feeling rested and refreshed, remembering my exciting caveman adventure. I thought of how tired my starving host was after running half a day to track down the wooly mammoth, and then hauling the heavy load back to the cave.

I felt no fatigue after waking up from the adventure. That's one of the good things about my time travels; my physical body suffers no residual effects from the experience. I can never be harmed, regardless of how dangerous my adventure is. My body stays in my bed, getting a good night's sleep. It's only my spirit or aura, vapor, or whatever you want to call it that enters the host's body. I experience his life through him. I become him. I don't harm him in any way and he doesn't know I'm there. I'm only there to observe. I can't influence his behavior in any way

I don't know exactly how all this time travel stuff works, not yet anyway. Doctor Magas—or Grampa, as I'm trying to learn to call him, does all the navigating. For now, I'm only visiting exciting times and places and getting a good understanding of what happened back then.

My new grandfather has exposed me to so much since we met a couple of months ago. Who would have ever thought that I would be taking these unbelievable time-travel adventures? This whole concept is fantastic. I'm anxious to learn so much more of this bizarre new power I apparently have. To do that, I must spend more time with my grandfather and really become his apprentice.

Even though it's school vacation, there are no skipping chores around the house. Saturday mornings are usually reserved for working with Dad, taking care of the house and yard. I got up, dressed and met him in the kitchen where he was drinking coffee and reading the morning paper.

"Morning Champ," he said looking up from the paper. "You sleep okay?"

"Oh yeah, fine. Hope I didn't sleep in too late. Celebrating summer vacation, I guess."

"No, you deserve it. We'll get to work on the yard soon enough. You get some breakfast. You'll need your energy today."

"Why? What are we gonna do?"

"Before your mom left for the grocery store, she showed me where she wants that new flower bed for roses that she's been talking about. I thought we'd jump on that today. It shouldn't take more than a couple of hours or so. You get some breakfast while I gather the tools and I'll meet you out back."

After a quick breakfast of cereal, fruit, and juice, I met Dad in the backyard and got busy measuring the flower bed location, driving stakes in the ground, and stringing line between the stakes. Then we took turns breaking up the soil with the garden turning fork.

I enjoyed my Saturday mornings with Dad. It was our time together, just the two of us. We talked about anything and everything. I looked forward to that time with him.

"Dad," I said, "have you ever wondered what it would be like to live back in the cave man's time?"

He stopped digging and leaned on the gardening fork, smiling at me. "No, I don't guess I've really given it much thought. Why?"

"Well, I got another book from Doc, I mean Grampa, to read over the summer. It's all about the people that explored this part of the world back in the old days. It covers everything from stone-age men to people that opened up the American West. I read the first chapter last night. It was about people that came here from Asia on a land bridge. They eventually spread all over North and South America."

"That's a very interesting story," Dad said, pushing the garden fork into the soil, turning another clump of dirt. "You know when that migration first started, it was still the Ice Age. Those early people must have had it pretty tough."

"They sure did," I said, remembering my adventure from just a few hours earlier.

Dad looked at me and nodded. "You know that migration took tens of thousands of years. There were climatic changes during that time that caused much of the country that had been covered in ice to thaw and become a good environment for both animals and man. Those people became today's Native Americans. They had a very long history of exploring and trailblazing as generation after generation moved around, settling in different areas as they followed the large animals they depended on for food."

I looked back to see how we were progressing on our project and realized we were already over half-way done turning the soil and cleaning out the vegetation. The rest of the work; digging and cleaning the grass didn't take much longer. While I finished picking the last of the grass from the dirt, Dad took the wheelbarrow and brought three bags of peat moss from the garage. We dumped the moss into the flower bed and mixed it in with the dirt. After mixing it well, we bagged the grass and roots we pulled from the dirt, removed the stakes and line used to design the bed and stepped back to admire our work.

"I'm sure your mom will be proud of that," Dad said. "Thanks, Max. Good job. I expect when Mom sees this, she'll want to run down to the nursery and get a bunch of rose bushes to plant. I know what I'll be doing the rest of the afternoon."

"Will you need me to help?" I knew that most kids would want to get out of stuff like planting roses, but I kinda liked working with the dirt. I guess it came naturally since both Mom and Dad liked gardening. Dad had always taught me to take pride in the way our yard looked.

"No, you've done enough," he said. "You're always lots of help to me. I appreciate it. You go enjoy your day. I'll take it from here."

I helped him put the tools and trash away, went inside and took a shower to wash the dirt and sweat off. After changing clothes, I went downstairs to find that Dad had made sandwiches for lunch.

"So, what's on your agenda for the rest of the day," he asked as I dug into the turkey sandwich and chips.

"I haven't had a good bike ride in a while. I thought I'd go see if Rick or Jeremy or both of 'em want to join me for a ride around town. Might be gone a few hours."

"That's fine. Don't let Rick talk you into any daredevil stunts on your bike. You don't want to be wearing a cast like he did last summer."

I laughed. "You know, Dad, Jeremy and I have an understanding. Whenever Rick suggests something that's a little outside the realm of sanity, we veto it. He may go ahead and do it while we watch. It's okay if he calls us 'little old ladies, afraid of our own shadow,' but so far, we've never broken any bones taking him up on dares for his knucklehead schemes. He's a little goofy sometimes, but he's still a good guy. He sorta needs me and Jeremy to kinda look after him to keep him from getting seriously hurt."

"Well, he's lucky to have you as friends.

"Oh, I almost forgot," he added, "your mom and I were talking this morning before you got up about our camping trip plans. If it's okay with you, we'd like to ask your grandfather to come along with us. We talked to Megan about it before she went to her Saturday job. She thinks it a great idea. After all, it is a family camping trip. He's now part of the family. We'll have plenty of room with the extra tent we bought last year. If you happen to be close to downtown on your ride, you may want to stop by his place and see if he'd like to join us next weekend."

"I think it's a great idea," I grinned. "It will give us all a good chance to get better acquainted."

Before I headed out the door, dad reached into his back pocket, pulled out his wallet and handed me a ten-dollar bill. "Thanks for all the help you give me and your mom. Take this. You and your friends might get thirsty on your ride."

"Thanks," I said, grinning and stuffed the bill into my pocket. Mom and Dad don't give me a regular allowance, but almost every week one or the other of them give me a few dollars for the little jobs I do. Seldom do I have to ask for money. If I do, it's usually for some kind of school fee.

Soon I was out on my bicycle rounding up my friends. I rode up Rick's driveway and rang the doorbell when I remembered him saying something earlier in the week about his dad taking him to the stock car races this weekend. Sure enough, when his mother came to the door, she verified that he just left with his dad to go pick up his uncle and cousin to head over to the races. Oh well, I'll just go on over to Jeremy's and see if he wants to take a ride.

When I pulled up in their yard, Jeremy and his little brother were helping their dad load his truck with fishing gear.

"Hey Max," Jeremy called over his shoulder. He and his dad lifted a big blue cooler onto the truck bed, "What's up?"

"Aw, I was just getting' a little ride in. Thought I'd see if you want to go. Looks like you have fishing on your mind, though."

"Yeah, Dad's taking Boomer and me out to the river to drown some worms."

His seven-year-old brother, they called Boomer, handed his dad his kid's fishing rod to stow in the truck bed. "I'm gonna catch the biggest one," he said, 'cause I got a secret fishin' recipe that my Grampa showed me."

"What's that?" I asked.

"Wouldn't be secret if I told you, would it?" He turned to go back to the garage for his tackle box.

Jeremy's dad chuckled and lowered his voice to explain. "He remembers the time his Grampa spit on a worm before throwing his line in the river and caught a good-sized catfish. He calls it Grampa's fishin' recipe."

"Who knows," I said, "maybe it works."

"Dad," Jeremy asked, "can Max go with us?"

"Sure, we've got plenty of room," Jeremy's dad said. "Max, you wanna go fishing?"

"Oh, thanks, Mister Elliott, but there's somebody I have to see while I'm out on my ride. How about next time?"

"Anytime. We've got extra gear too. Maybe your dad would like to join us next time too."

"I know he'd like that. I'll tell him. See ya later. Good luck with the fishing."

I got back on my bike and took off down the street. It had been a long time since I'd spent the afternoon riding my bike around town by myself. When I was younger, about nine or ten, hardly a week went by in the summer that I wasn't out riding for hours. Sometimes with the guys, sometimes without.

I headed in a round-about way into town and rode to the courthouse square. I wanted to stop by Grampa's place and tell him about the camping trip but didn't want to show up hungry. The sandwich I had earlier was beginning to wear off. Since the ice cream store was on the other side of the square, I walked my bike along the sidewalks, looking in the shop windows as I headed around for a cold treat. When I reached the ice cream shop, I went inside and ordered a double dip vanilla cone.

After being served, I walked my bike across the street to the bench on the courthouse lawn.

That's where I had gotten acquainted with Doctor Magas, who I now know as my grandfather. We had several meetings there talking about his powers as a real magician, time travel, and the lost books of discovery.

As I sat eating my ice cream, trying not to let it melt and drip onto my shoes, I thought about the talks we had together.

I've learned so much since I met him. I've already taken time-travel trips into the very early days in Texas to learn how the Indians lived before white people complicated their lives. I also followed the progress of white settlers in Texas as they made their homes and fought for independence from Mexico. Now I'm learning about the exciting exploration in America. I shook my head at how impossible it all seemed.

My mind drifted back to the time he told me about his background.

"You know, Max," he said, "my family had a terrible reputation in the old country. They were gypsies, which I had no problem with, but they were also thieves and scoundrels. I had a big problem with that. Their crimes and reputation cost me my one and only love, your grandmother, when her father shipped her and her mother away to America to keep her from marrying me.

So, as a broken-hearted young man, I left my family to their thieving ways and dedicated my life to study and advancing my career in science, historical research, archeology, and the magic within me. The study of my ancestors to better understand the extent of their magical powers led me to fantastic discoveries.

"So, that's how it all got started for you?"

"Yes, pretty much. What I found was really exciting. I found that some of the early ancestors were brilliant scientists of their day as well as powerful magicians. Through persistent digging, I learned that some of their secret experiments led to advanced scientific discoveries. Many of those discoveries were well ahead of their time. Some were decades, if not centuries ahead of even our current-day science. Society of their time was far from being ready for those discoveries.

"Max, those early scientists were wise enough to carefully hide their documents. As those ancestor magician/scientists died, their hidden discoveries were lost. Many of those papers and the fortunes in scientific research they contain have been lost for centuries.

"But through diligence and hard work over the years, I've been able to find some of those ancient books and other important artifacts. Once the papers were translated, I learned how important, powerful and valuable their documented discoveries are."

I remember him leaning toward me on this bench and lowering his voice to almost a whisper. He said, "If some of the science contained in those documents fell into the wrong hands and was used inappropriately by evil forces to satisfy personal greed or to achieve power, it could spell *disaster*, perhaps even *doom* for our world.

"However," he said, holding his finger beside his nose, "if harnessed successfully in the future, when the science of that time is ready, those discoveries could tremendously improve the way people live and the world as a whole.

"Max, just imagine no more hunger or poverty, worldwide. Think of major diseases eradicated. Think of exploring the universe without distance and time restrictions. Those are only a few of the things that could be accomplished when modern science is ready for those hidden discoveries. That's why I search for them and protect them."

I sat and thought about all the cool stuff that could happen when science catches up with Grampa's discoveries. I guess he really is the keeper and guardian of those ancient documents and the secrets that goes with them. That's gotta be a big job; taking care of all that like he does. I wonder where they are. I just hope there aren't any bad guys out there looking for them. Disaster and doom sound pretty scary.

CHAPTER 4

I remember the first-time Mom, Dad, Megan, and I saw Grampa's place. We were in awe of how beautiful he'd made it. When he found us and moved to our town, he bought one of the grand old homes in one of the historical sections, close to downtown that was built in the 1890's by a wealthy businessman. It had been vacant for several years and had become run down. He totally remodeled the old place inside and out and created a fantastic garden on the property.

When I rode onto the empty driveway, I was impressed again with the beauty of the grounds surrounding the home. Obviously, it took a lot of work to create and maintain all the flower gardens along the house foundation and clustered around the huge trees in the yard.

"Hello." I heard a man's voice call from the side yard. When I looked, I saw a man in his early-forties pushing himself up from his knees beside a flower bed. He looked like he had been weeding and working the dirt. A couple of partially filled black trash bags and a bag of fertilizer sat beside him along with some garden tools. A welcoming smile crossed his face as he walked toward me. I lowered the bike's kickstand and watched him approach. He was a big man—over six feet tall. He looked like he worked out a lot. His full, curly blond beard and hair looked to be the same length—a little over an inch long. Although he was intimidating looking, his friendly approach put me at ease.

"Hi, I'm Mike Hatcher. My friends call me Hatch." His smile broadened as he reached to shake my hand. "I work for Doctor Magas. You must be Max."

"Yeah—uh, yes, I am. How'd you know?"

"Oh, you ought to hear the way the Doctor talks about you and your family. He's very proud of you, you know. He was so pleased when he got the invitation to go meet your family for the first time."

"Is he here?"

"Oh, yes. I'm sure he'll be happy to see you. He's around back in his studio. Let's go this way." He turned and walked beside me along a garden path that looped its way through the side yard alongside the multi-colored flower beds toward the back of the property.

Hatch reached to his belt as we walked and pulled out a small two-way radio. He put it to his lips and spoke. "Three to one."

In a couple of seconds, a voice answered. "Go ahead." It was Doctor Magas' voice.

"You have a guest," Hatch said on the radio.

"Who?"

"Young Max just rode up on his bicycle."

"Wonderful! Bring him on out."

I smiled at hearing the pleasure in my grandfather's voice to learn that I'd dropped in on him.

We passed the outdoor entertainment area where my family had dinner with him just a couple of weeks ago. It was a wonderful night. That was when we learned he was my mom's father and my grandfather.

Grampa's studio was at the back of the large, corner lot, beside a three-car garage. The studio was as large as many houses. Both it and the garage were finished on the outside with the same stone as the big house. Hatch opened the door and ushered me in and excused himself.

I was welcomed with my grandfather's big smile and open arms. I'd never seen him smile so big. He seemed genuinely happy to see me. He shook my hand and wrapped his other arm around me, drawing me close. "What a nice surprise," he said stepping back to look at me. "I'm so glad to see you. What brought you by today?"

"I was out for a bike ride and wanted to stop by and say hi. Also, we want to invite you to go camping with us for a long weekend next Thursday. We'll leave Thursday afternoon and come back Monday. There's a fun state park we like on the river that's great for fishing and hiking. Mom and Dad said you don't have to bring anything except your clothes. We have everything else you need. You can sleep in the tent with me and Dad. I hope you don't have other plans."

"If I had other plans, I'd certainly cancel them for an opportunity like that. I've never gone camping with my family. Yes, I'd be thrilled to go. Now certainly there's more I can bring than just a sleeping bag."

"I guess you can work that out with Mom. She wants you to call her to let her know if you can come."

"Great, I'll do that tonight. Thank you so much for the invitation. Now, let me show you around the studio."

My head swiveled as I looked around the big open area loaded with work tables, power tools, and a huge assortment of hand tools.

"You remember when your mother asked what I do for hobbies in addition to painting? I told her I like most of the creative arts. Here," he said, stretching his arms out wide, "is where I play." We slowly walked to the center of the large room where he pointed out all the hobbies he could carry out in his studio. "Over here by the big window on this wall to your left is where I do my drawing and painting. There's good light here."

Next to the painting area was a countertop with cabinets and sink along the wall. A workbench ran parallel to the cabinet area. "This is where I do my sculpture work."

Then we turned to face the back wall. "Back here is the hot area. I can use the kiln for processing everything from pottery to jewelry. Next is the blast furnace for working glass. Then there's the blacksmith station with the furnace, anvil, and supplies for working steel. Next is the welding shop with all the gasses, torches, clamps, and stands I need."

He turned to his right and gestured toward all the flat-topped work surfaces, tool boxes, and power equipment on stands. "Most of this over here is for woodworking and carving.

"Notice that each work area has its own cluster of lighting from the ceiling." He also pointed out the multiple vacuum outlets throughout the room that made it easy for fast cleanup. We completed the circuit of the clean, well-organized studio and stood next to a booth in the corner.

"This area here is separated from the rest of the room so it can be kept especially clean for spray painting. It also has its own special exhaust system."

He turned and gestured toward the back part of the shop. "Back here is where I'm working today." I followed him as he walked back through the array of equipment toward the rear of the room. We stopped at a workbench loaded with small hand and power tools. There was also a set of gas torches with cylinders strapped to the backside of the table. A ten-inch round magnifying glass with a built-in light reached above the center of the bench by an adjustable arm from its stand. It was a jeweler's workbench.

He sat on the stool at the workbench and nodded toward a close-by stool. "Pull up that stool so you can see what I'm doing." I put the stool next to him and sat. "I was working on this when Hatch called to say you were here."

Sitting in the middle of his workbench was a chunk of what looked like hard wax. He picked it up, holding it in one hand and started carving on it with a sharp instrument in the other. "I just have a few more details to complete while they are fresh in my mind.

"What are you working on?" I asked, now curious about the object he held, partially obscured to me by his hand.

"Oh, it's a piece of jewelry," he said as he trimmed away minuscule pieces of wax with the small carving instrument. "You see, I carve the piece in the wax the way it will look as a finished product. Then I make a mold around the carved wax piece. When the mold is ready, I pour melted gold or silver into the mold. The hot gold melts the wax, replacing the wax with the metal. When the gold turns solid again, the mold can be removed and the object will be trimmed, polished and finished. It's called the lost wax process. The work is very soothing. You'll have to watch me sometimes through the whole procedure. Maybe you'd like to make something yourself."

"I'd like that," I said. "It sounds fun. You know, Mom's birthday is next month. Maybe we can make something for her."

"We can do that, but she's not the only one to have a birthday soon. Yours is coming up in a few days. As I recall, your birthday is next weekend, while we'll be camping."

"Yeah, I guess it is."

"There. That's it," he said as he flicked a couple of small pieces of wax away with his instrument and blew some smaller ones from the object he held in his hand. That's enough of that for today." He wrapped the wax object in a soft cloth and put it on the table.

"Tell me, Max, why are you out riding your bike alone? I would imagine that you'd have lots of friends to spend your time with during the summer."

"Oh, I do, a couple anyway. I usually go riding with Rick and Jeremy. They were both busy with their families today. But I enjoy riding alone sometimes. It gives me time to think."

"So, what does a young, carefree guy like you have to think about on a summer day like today?"

"Well, lately, I'm thinking more and more about the time travel stuff."

A set of worry lines developed around Grampa's eyes.

"Are you having difficulty with it?"

"No, not at all. Just the opposite. I'm fascinated by it. I want to do more. I want to learn more. So far, it's been just one exciting adventure after another, and I'm learning so much. But I want to help you. If there are bad guys out there looking for those lost books to use for evil purposes, shouldn't I be trying to help you find some before they do?"

"I'll admit there's plenty to do. I've found that it's not only just our ancestors that left undiscovered treasures. Hundreds of others through the ages have made noteworthy and sometimes extremely valuable contributions to science and the arts that have yet to be discovered. Those are also included in our findings. But I can only do so much myself. No one, except me and my blood relatives has the ability to do what you and I are doing. You will be helping me in time, when you're ready."

"Are you sure I have any power?" I asked. "I sure don't feel powerful."

"I'm absolutely positive you do," he smiled and winked at me. "That's why I brought you into my confidence. Your magic is in your genes. You haven't been trained yet as to how to use it to its fullest advantage. You wouldn't be having your exciting adventures if you didn't possess the power. It's always been there. We'll access it fully in time. Do you understand?"

"Yes, I guess I do," I said feeling a bit embarrassed. "I'm sorry for my impatience."

"Ah, the eagerness of youth," he said smiling and patting me on the shoulder. If only it could last a lifetime!"

"Well," I said getting up from the stool, "I don't want to interfere with your day. I just wanted to stop by and let you know about the camping trip. Thanks for showing me around your studio."

"You're welcome. I'm really looking forward to spending time with all of you in the woods. I'll talk to your mother tonight and get the details." He got up and escorted me to his studio door.

"Don't be a stranger to stopping by and visiting," he said as I followed the rock path back around to the front of the house.

Hatch waved at me from his work as I returned to my bike.

This is going to be a really fun summer, I grinned as I pushed away from his driveway and headed home.

CHAPTER 5

The next several days passed quickly as I helped Mom with a couple of projects around the house in the mornings and hung out with the guys in the afternoons. One day, the guys and I spent the afternoon shagging balls at the city park, then cooled down for an hour or so at the community swimming pool. Rick made a fool of himself as always, showing off in front of the girls on the diving board while Jeremy and I enjoyed relaxing in the cool water. Jeremy always gave me a hard time because I had to slather so much sunblock all over because of my fair skin.

"Hey man, you're creating an oil slick around you," he said. Now if you had nice chocolate skin like mine, you wouldn't need so much of that stuff. Your skin color would just get a little richer in the sun."

"Well, I don't, and all mine does is just get redder, blister, and peel without all this stuff, so back off," I said playfully, splashing a double handful of water on his face. Soon we had an all-out water splashing fight with Rick joining us by jumping in right next to us with a super big belly flop. We created quite a ruckus, sending water into the air all around until the high school kid, sitting in the lifeguard tower, blew his whistle and told us to stop. After an hour or so enjoying the cool pool, we were water-logged and grabbed our bikes and headed home.

That night, the night before we left for our camping trip, was the next time I picked up the big explorer book. I knew I wouldn't have a chance to read while on the outing with the family, so I wanted to get another adventure in before we left. I got in bed and opened it again to the table of contents. The chapters and adventures were listed in the order that they happened, with the story of the stone-age people first. I nestled in on my belly and started reading the next chapter.

The Vikings

The early Viking's were fierce warriors and feared by their enemies. They were also shipbuilders and adventures that explored and waged war over much of the coastlines of the North Atlantic and the seas around northwestern Europe. Many of them made their homes in present-day Norway.

Sometime about 1000 AD, groups led by Eric the Red and his son Leif Eriksson settled in Iceland and later in Greenland.

The Viking's curious nature and bravery on the seas led them to explore further west where they discovered the northeast portions of North America.

Suddenly I saw and felt the now familiar tiny sparkles and powder-like dust emitting from the book marker and settling over me. I left my sleeping body on the bed and started making my reverse journey through time. The flickering images were always interesting, showing fleeting views of the past. I watched as they moved backward at a tremendous rate of speed. The images finally reduced their speed and came to a stop. It was a time when Vikings took to the sea.

The stinging slap of cold seawater across my face made me realize that I had again taken human form.

"Pull men, pull! Give it all you've got! Put your backs into it," Leif Eriksson bellowed from the stern of the ship. His words were barely understood by us as they were ripped away by the howling winds and the constant torrent of cold sea water and rain that drenched us all. He strained against the tiller as he guided us through the storm.

"Heave hard to port, lads! Starboard—backstroke—now!" he yelled, using us, his oarsmen to assist the rudder, steering the vessel into the oncoming waves. We knew that if we allowed the boat to become parallel with the rollers, we'd be swamped in a trough between the massive, crashing waves and lost forever. Leif kept up a constant barrage of calling for more effort and adjustments to our stroke as we strained every muscle, over and over again, pulling on the heavy oars, moving and adjusting the position of the longboat through the violent, foamy sea.

I squinted to see through the mixed sea water and rain moving sideways through the howling wind trying to locate my father's boat. There was nothing but rain and blowing water above the ocean surface as far as I could see, which wasn't far at all.

There were two boats on our voyage. My father was the master of our number two boat. It should have been somewhere to our right. My older brother, Ansgar, was an oarsman on our father's boat. I was sure they were having as much trouble as we were dealing with the angry sea.

The action that my host body was involved in was so intense, I fell immediately into the work and started understanding who, what, where and when I was.

I was Holgar, son of Gunhild. I was a sixteen-year-old Viking youth taking part in my first major adventure at sea. The time was summer. The place was many days voyage west of Iceland, in the middle of a very nasty storm. I was one of the eighteen oarsmen— nine to a side in the longboat. As always, I had become a part of my host. I knew everything about him. I knew all of his memories and his hopes and dreams. I was him. At that very moment, all I could hope for was that we could all survive that hellish storm. Although I stayed alert to Leif's commands to help push the boat through the waves and responded to his orders, my mind wandered to what brought us there.

I remembered the clan meeting that spring when we all gathered around the council house fire. Leif called the meeting. He's the head man of our clan. His smile shined through his thick beard as he looked around the dimly-lit longhouse at his family and friends. Except for a few of the old among us, we were healthy and strong. Several babies had been born during the dark days of winter. We'd all had enough to eat that year. Our hunts on the ice for seal, sea lion and walrus had been successful. We'd also been lucky enough to bring in caribou and other game several times during the winter. Recently, with warmer weather and the ice breaking up, we were able to use our nets for fishing.

We always gathered in the log council house when we had news to share or to plan a hunt or a war expedition. Sometimes we held feasts there to celebrate a good hunt or raiding campaign. I wondered about the purpose of this meeting.

Leif waited until those around him settled onto their polar bear, sea lion or caribou robes on the floor and quieted. Soon he saw that we were all eager to listen to what he had to say.

"Friends and family, the Gods have smiled on us this year. We've once again made it through the hard winter. Our needs have been met. The hunts have been good and our last raid before winter brought most of our men home safely, along with our plunder. We spent our winter wisely. Not only have our hunts provided food for our families, we've made our old boats like new and finished a new one.

"Now the cold, dark days of winter are gone. The animals are moving about, hungry from the hard winter, looking to take advantage of what the warmer days bring. The birds have spread their wings and taken flight with the new season; flying far away, looking to see what the future holds for them."

He hesitated, taking a deep breath and allowing a broad smile to cross his face. "As Vikings, we must do the same. We must do as we always do. We must go and see what good fortune will bring us." He looked anxious and excited to share his news.

"This time, we will test ourselves and go where we've never been. Instead of challenging the Celts, Normans, or Saxons in the familiar old world, we'll sail west, following the sun into the unknown. Like our fathers sailed west and found this land, we must do the same. There certainly must be more land out to the west. And who knows, there may be riches beyond belief there as well. We won't know until we explore. There may be challenges thrown at us, and they may be harsh. But we're Vikings." He raised his sword high over his head and shouted, "We'll fight our way through anything!"

His words, and the resulting cheering, echoed through my mind as I pulled with all my might on the oar, responding to his commands. So far, we'd managed to keep our boat heading into the wind, riding the massive waves to avoid disaster. We'd been battling the storm most of the day, fighting to keep from being swamped by the huge waves. At least it was still daylight and we had a little ability to see the waves rolling toward us through the driving wind and rain. *How will we see when darkness falls?*

We took the big, square sail down mid-morning and secured it when the wind first started buffeting the boat. We'd been on the oars ever since. Our direction of travel on the sea mattered little now. The only direction we concerned ourselves with was into the wind. We'd redirect our course after we rode out the storm.

I thought about my father and brother on the other boat somewhere out there. I had no way of knowing if they were still alive.

I remember working with my father and brother, packing the boats with supplies before we left home. I had just learned that I would be on Leif's crew and not my father's. I turned to my father, Gunhild, and talked quietly so Leif wouldn't overhear.

"But I want to be on your boat with you and Ansgar."

He pulled me aside on the beach, away from the boats for a private talk.

"Son," he said quietly, "you are assigned to my friend Leif's boat because I asked him to include you in his crew. He's not only the leader of our clan, he's the best sailor, navigator, and bravest warrior I know. I'll trust my son to him anytime, under any circumstance. If you ever get in trouble, he's the man I want by your side. Holgar, you're my second son. Your older brother and I are in the same boat. If anything should happen to our boat and us, I want you to survive. If we had three boats on this voyage, I'd put your brother on the third boat. Do you understand?"

I nodded sheepishly. I was ashamed that I had questioned the wisdom of my father or Leif. I knew I had much to learn.

My brothers and I played and practiced war games all the years we were growing up and our father tested us from time to time with the bow and arrow, lance, shield, and sword. Although I'd never been tested in battle, I was confident that I could stand up to any man. My father had seen to that with my training. Vikings are tall, so being only sixteen-years-old, my father told me I was as large or larger and stronger than most men I would face in battle. I was ready to fight.

I wished I felt as confident about the sea. Although my brothers and I had launched small boats and rafts around the inlets and bay back home and I'd been on fishing and hunting trips with father in the longboat, I'd never been on the open sea in a raging storm with huge waves and howling wind.

After so many hours of fighting the waves, they became almost predictable as to when they would roll toward us. All we could do was steel our bodies to the stinging rain and steer the bow straight into them.

First, we cut into the swell. Then the upsurge threw the bow high into the air, over the top and slammed us back down the backside of the breaker into the trough. Occasionally a rogue surge surprised us; curling through much larger and more powerful than the ones before, grasping, twisting and tugging at us, almost as if it had taken a life of its own, attempting to throw us under. Each time, somehow, we fought our way through.

Frequently, after the big wave encounters, I found myself visualizing the image of Leif after he told our clan of his plan for this voyage, standing with his sword held high over his head shouting, "We'll fight our way through anything!" That image gave me the strength to carry on.

This morning before the storm, I marked twenty-eight days on the water. I cut another notch on a stick that I brought aboard for keeping track of our days on the journey. I'll have space enough for about a hundred notches on the stick. *How many sticks will I collect and fill with notches before we return home?*

We'd enjoyed favorable winds and fair skies most days. We'd seen little on the water during our journey except for pieces of floating ice and frequent large icebergs. We'd also spotted a few whales. Yesterday our spirits were raised when we saw a flock of birds. *Could land be close with birds overhead?*

Our fair weather and calm seas ran out this morning with heavy dark clouds to the south. We knew that to be a sign of approaching bad weather, so we prepared for the storm as best we could. We tied down all loose gear and ate from our limited stores before the weather hit. We didn't know how long it would be before we had another chance for a meal.

As best as I could tell, we'd been maintaining a southwestern course all day, fighting the oncoming wind, rain, and waves. The little amount of daylight that filtered through the driving rain was almost gone. It was going to be a really dark night. It seemed like we'd been rowing for days instead of hours.

How much longer can we do this? My arms felt so heavy. Each stroke seemed so much harder to do than the last. But we all worked together—all oars moving as one. We kept our heads down most of the time, staring at the deck under our feet, avoiding the sting of the cold rain.

I shifted in my seat and straightened my back, stretched my legs to avoid a cramp, and looked up into the wet murkiness.

What's that? I blinked to clear the salt water from my eyes. It was a dim contrast of colors—a light horizontal line with dark shapes above. *Can it be? Is it really? It is!*

I yelled loud as I could, "Land Ho! Surf on rocks! Eighty paces starboard!" I looked at Leif and pointed. "We're almost on the rocks!"

Leif shielded his eyes from the rain with his hand and saw what I saw. He leaned hard on the tiller and started shouting orders. We all forgot our fatigue and responded like a machine to his commands.

Our boat had a shallow draft, but we had no idea just how shallow the water was. We could crash against underwater rocks at any moment. Powering our strokes with just the right timing to put the ship at the top of the waves at precisely the right moment took extraordinary teamwork. To ride over the waves *and* propel the craft away from rocks without getting caught sideways in a trough took skill, daring, and a crew that worked together flawlessly.

I had to remind myself to breathe as we pulled together, working our way out of that jam. It took several minutes, but we got the boat away from the rocks. But we weren't out of trouble.

We were safely into deeper water, but we were still in a raging storm and couldn't see well at all. The farther, and safer away from land we sailed, the less we could see the coastline. Darkness now presented a new set of problems.

We needed to find safe harbor. To do that, we needed to see the coastline. To see the coastline, we must be closer to shore. To get closer, we could be dashed into the rocks.

Soon, the approaching darkness brought us a welcome surprise. The intensity of the wind lessened after dark, reducing the size of the waves. The rain also slackened to a drizzle, allowing us a little better visibility. We couldn't see much into the murkiness, but we could at least see the contrast of the white surf against the rocks from a safe distance.

We rowed several hours into the night, following the coastline south until it made a turn west into what we later discovered was a small harbor. We were finally out of the wind and the killer waves. *And* we had just discovered a new land!

Nobody, however, was in a mood to celebrate that night. We didn't know what had happened to my father and brother and the rest of their crew, and I worried about their welfare. We stayed aboard the boat all night, anchored in the harbor. None of us were foolish enough to want to venture onto an unknown shore in the middle of the night. We needed daylight to learn what hazards would confront us on this unknown shore.

That night was more wet, cold, and miserable than any of the other twenty-seven nights since we'd left home. Even food didn't lift our spirits. The only provisions we had left that hadn't spoiled or was ruined by seawater was smoked caribou meat.

I didn't sleep much because of worrying about my father and brother and wondering what we'd find ashore after daylight. The rain stopped sometime during the early morning hours and the wind calmed.

CHAPTER 6

I must have dozed off at some point because I woke to gentle waves lapping at a sandy beach and birds calling in the distance. My eyelids were swollen and almost stuck together and my eyes burned from so much exposure to salt water. I blinked several times to try to clear them to see a heavy fog hanging over the bay. The sun was barely up, casting a subtle, pink glow through the fog, giving our entire surroundings a strange pastel look. I could only see far enough through the fog to the dense stand of trees beyond the beach, about eighty paces from where we were anchored.

Some of the other men were waking up and moving about. One started to speak but was immediately stopped by "shhh!" I looked up to find the source of the hiss and saw that it came from Leif, standing at the stern. He pressed his finger to his lips, signaling for quiet. He cocked his head to the side with his eyes closed tightly. He shook his other hand, fingers outstretched, pointing toward the other side of the bay. He'd heard something.

Then I heard it myself. It sounded like wood against wood. A piece of wood had been dropped against another. Then it happened again. There was no mistaking it.

Sounds traveled on still water for long distances. The presence of fog also amplifies sound. We had no idea how far the sounds were from us, but it was definitely on the other side of the bay. Someone or some *thing* was over there.

Everyone was now awake, alert, and watching Leif for orders. He whispered, moving his lips in an exaggerated way, and using hand signals. "Check your weapons and keep them close, ready for use." He slung his quiver of arrows over his shoulder, put his bow and shield within arm's reach, and hoisted his sword in the air to show he was ready for battle. We all followed his example, preparing our weapons.

He moved to mid-ship to allow us all to hear better. "Be very careful. You must be absolutely quiet," he whispered. "Prepare to cast off." He held his hands chest high, palms out to reinforce his order, "Make no noise." We positioned our oars in their swivels, grasping them firmly, awaiting his order. "Weigh anchor," he whispered. Two men carefully and silently drew the rope to bring the anchor from the bay floor, stowed it in the bow and took their positions at their oars.

Leif returned to the stern, took hold of the tiller with one hand and raised the other over his head. He held his fist over his head momentarily, whispered, "slowly and quietly," then lowered his hand, fingers extended, to point straight ahead.

The water surface, in stark contrast to the way it was the night before, was calm; almost like a mirror. The longboat moved silently through the water, leaving only a quiet ripple in its wake. Our oars sliced through the surface with each careful stroke, leaving only tiny droplets as they arced above the water like dolphins breaking the surface for another soft stroke.

Leif strained his eyes and his ears to look and listen through the dense fog, adjusting the tiller only slightly as he guided the ship into the unknown. We all acted as lookouts with Leif, listening to pinpoint our target through the fog. We heard it again. It sounded like logs being dropped into a pile. Now it sounded like it was to our left. It was louder. We were close. Suddenly the shoreline came into view through the fog. We'd made it to the opposite side of the small bay. We scanned the shoreline as it became clearer through the now thinning fog. We saw nothing but thick forest beyond the sandy but rock-strewn beaches. If the fog thinned much more, we'd lose our cover.

The last sounds we heard were to our left. Leif adjusted our course so that we were slowly paralleling the shoreline, about a hundred paces from the water's edge, moving deeper into the bay. The fog continued thinning, revealing more of the empty beach as it slid by to our right.

A point of land jutted out in front of us. It extended the shoreline another hundred and fifty paces or so. Leif adjusted his steering to curve around the point, keeping his distance from possible underwater rocks.

Suddenly the hairs stood up on the back of my neck. Faint voices and the smell wood smoke hung in the fog. I couldn't make anything of the voices. Still too far away. I looked at the men around me. They heard and smelled it too. There's a look that warriors get immediately before facing the enemy. Those men had that look. It was a look of determination. They were ready to kill.

I hoped I was too. I glanced at my weapons. I rehearsed in my mind how I'd put the oar in its lock, grab my weapons and take to one knee, ready to let my arrows fly when given the command. My eyes were riveted on the edge of the water at the point of land, just ahead. I could see nothing beyond that point but water and fog. Then the bow of our boat silently slid past the point.

Sixty paces ahead of us and nosed into the sandy beach was my father's ship. He, my brother and their crew were warming themselves and drying their clothes around a blazing fire.

I expelled a huge sigh of relief as Leif called, "Ahoy, Gunhild!" We were all joyously shouting back and forth until Leif got our attention to bring our boat around and nose into the beach, next to the other.

I scrambled from the boat and ran to my father and brother. They met me with their arms outstretched.

"I didn't know if I'd ever see you again," I said as we embraced.

"Oh, I had no such concerns," my father scoffed. You were in Leif's boat. I knew he'd see you through. He and I have weathered storms like that in the North Sea. He knew what he was doing."

Our reunion was joyful as we slapped our friends and family on the backs, congratulating each other for the good fortune of surviving the storm and finding the previously undiscovered land. There was much to be happy about that morning.

Soon Leif divided the men into several groups. Two small units of the best hunters were sent into the woods in different directions to find food and learn the lay of the land. The rest of us busied ourselves making repairs to the boats that were caused by the storm and making simple shelters. It appeared that we would be spending at least one night there.

By early afternoon the hunters returned with two fat deer and three large and strange looking, but delicious birds. It was enough to feed the entire group with a real feast and have plenty left over to smoke by the fire. By that evening, the shelters were built and the minor boat repairs were made. Several times during the day, I was distracted from my work by the aroma of the meat over the fire. That evening the whole company sat around several fires in dry clothes, relaxing, and enjoying the first fresh meat we'd tasted in a very long time.

After we'd eaten our fill, Leif stood to speak. He hesitated for a moment smiling, looking into the bearded faces that were brightened by the flickering flames of the fires. "Friends, you should be very proud of yourselves. Yesterday you not only showed your skill as sailors working so closely as a team, tirelessly and successfully fighting the storm as long as you did, but you found new land!

"Before we left home, we had no idea of what we'd find as we followed the sun to the west. I didn't know if we'd just find day after day of cold, deep water. I hoped we'd find land like our fathers did when they found the place we now call home.

"This is an exciting place. I have no way of knowing at this time just how big it is. We could be on an island like Iceland. Or we could have landed on the shore of a very large land. We'll not know until we explore. I can already see the resources are abundant. Look at the timber. Those fine trees are just waiting to be turned into lumber for shipbuilding or whatever we need. Our hunters found wildlife so plentiful, they had no trouble bringing in meat enough for a grand feast in such a short time. They also report plenty of wild fruit and nuts as well as many other eatables just waiting for the picking.

"They found something else of importance. We are not alone. Other people are here. They found a campfire not far away. It was only a couple of days old. At the fire site were animal bones—charred remains of a deer. We must be on constant alert. We know nothing of those people.

"We will stay here two days to rest and resupply with fresh water and food, then we'll explore."

I was excited about what the hunters found. What kind people lived in this place? All I'd seen was the rocky beach and a little of the woods beyond the water.

I'd only known the people in our clan. I'd never been with the warriors when they went on their raids to the old countries. I'd been told that people in other parts of the world were different from us. They didn't look like us and dressed in strange clothes. They even used a language we couldn't understand. Some of those people had treasures our warriors brought home after their successful raiding voyages. Mama still used iron pots that Papa brought from raids against the Celts. The sword and shield that Papa gave me were won in a battle against the Saxons. He said the warrior he got them from had no further use for them.

I spent part of the morning with several other men carrying empty pottery urns from the boats to a spring of fresh water we found.

Everyone was busy that evening. Of course, we all ate our fill of fresh meat. After our feast, some men tended the fires; slowly smoking and drying strips of meat for our travels. Others, including me, worked the animal hides. We used everything possible from the animals, including the brains for the hide tanning process. Usually, working hides was woman's work, but since there were no women with us, that task fell to the younger men.

When the work was done, the men started making preparations to sleep. I gathered my caribou hide to clear a space of twigs and rocks next to my father when Leif tapped me on the shoulder.

"You have late watch tonight. Tolgon will wake you early morning and you'll keep watch till daylight."

I nodded my understanding and looked past Leif to see Tolgon, another young man a little older than me, carrying his weapons toward the outer perimeter of the camp, into the woods, well beyond the firelight. Every young Viking knew the importance of being the eyes and ears of the camp while the rest of the warriors slept. We were trained since we were children that a good warning of danger if it presented itself was the only way we would survive if attacked by wild animals or the enemy. Being selected as a sentry was an honor because you were trusted to provide that protection. It was a role that was taken very seriously by every Viking.

I had no trouble falling asleep because of all the activities of the day and slept soundly until I felt the nudge at my feet.

"Wake up Holgar," Tolgon whispered. "It's your watch. All's quiet. Just the normal night sounds."

He waited next to me until he saw that I was awake, sitting up and reaching for my weapons and a small bag of dried meat before he moved away to his sleeping fur.

The fires had died to ashes over coals by then, leaving the camp almost as dark as the woods beyond the perimeter. I yawned, scratched my backside, and stretched as I walked around and between the sleeping men, picking my way carefully toward the edge of the woods. The last thing I wanted to do was to step on my elders in the middle of the night.

My eyes adjusted to the darkness of as I made my way from the rocky beach, farther into the trees beyond the camp. I knew where I would make my sentry's nest. I had identified it earlier, as soon as I was told I would have the late watch. Instead of going directly into the woods from the center of the camp, I moved to the right of the camp and sat at the base of a large rock that jutted up from the forest floor. With the rock to my back, I made no exposed silhouette, and my back was protected.

The night air was comfortable. It was approaching late summer. It had been warm earlier in the afternoon as we worked, but now a cool, quiet breeze came across camp from the water.

The sky was clear of clouds and moonless. The only light was from the stars. They gave me a minimal view of the camp. I had a clear view through the trees and underbrush to well beyond the far end of the camp. I focused on the dark canopy of trees. There was enough light to see the slight flutter of the leaves as the breeze drifted through them. At least I could see movement through the trees and in the camp.

I settled in and realized that it was comfortable enough to spend several hours leaning against the rock keeping an eye on the surrounding area until the sun woke the camp. I tested the placement location of my weapons. I wanted to make sure they were all within close reach for immediate use if needed. My sword and shield were on the ground to my right. My bow and eight arrows in the quiver were beside me to my left. I had wished for a helmet like my father, Leif, and some of the other elders wore, but I would have to earn the right to wear a metal helmet by showing bravery and fighting skill in battle.

Like Tolgon said, the only sounds were the normal summer night sounds. Crickets chirped, an occasional bird ruffled its feathers in its nest, a frog croaked by the distant creek, and the occasional spent, burnt log fell into the ashen coals at one of the campfires. A couple of times when I looked closely, I saw bats darting above the camp. They chased down their dinner of flying insects attracted to the animal hides drying by the fires.

I consciously tried to avoid allowing my mind to wander to absent-minded things; forcing my attention on the deep woods beyond the camp. Time moved ever so slowly through the dark night. Every few minutes I moved my head; looking into the darkness through the brush and trees, back and forth from the beach, beyond the camp, and back into the trees. Several times I got to my feet to stretch my body and investigate the area along the beach and trees beyond the other side of my rock.

I tracked time by watching stars move across the night sky. Locating a reference point where tree limbs crossed each other, and identifying stars that I knew, I followed their movement westward across the southern sky. I knew from the star's locations that dawn was approaching.

The eastern sky started slowly changing. The longer I watched, the more it changed from just a very slight lightness in the pitch dark to a dark gray in the sky.

Suddenly something changed. *What was that?* It took a second to register.

It was deathly quiet. All the night sounds abruptly stopped. No crickets. No frogs. A chill ran up my spine. The hair on my arms and the back of my neck stood up. I strained my eyes trying to see into the darkness. I swept across my entire field of vision looking for movement. Through the woods—nothing. Along the beach—nothing.

I turned my head and bent slightly to the left for my bow and arrows.

An arrow *whished* a half inch past the right side of my neck and clattered into the rock behind me, shattering into several pieces. One splintered arrow piece flew back and sliced a small furrow along my jaw.

"Warriors attacking!" I yelled. "They're in the woods." I grabbed my weapons and shoved myself off the ground.

Vikings bounded from their sleeping robes and grabbed their weapons to meet the attack. Within seconds, they'd formed a defensive line behind their strong, metal shields. I held my shield along my side, protecting my head and upper body as I raced to the defensive line. Several arrows bounced off the wall of shields as I dove onto the sand, between two men that opened a gap between their shields for me. In the dawn light of the woods, blurred figures ran toward us. They screamed war cries and released arrows and spears as they advanced against our line.

I had no idea who they were, where they came from, or why they were trying to kill us. It didn't matter. We were ready to fight. I looked through a crack between shields to see they were almost on us. What I saw registered in a split second. There were close to seventy men; almost two of them to one of us. About a third were running and screaming toward us. The rest were holding back. Some released arrows as they ran. Others waved war clubs with heavy rocks tied to the end. A few carried clubs that looked to have stone heads shaped like axes. Some carried stone-tipped spears. Everyone looked ferocious with their faces painted in bold designs with bright colored paint. Some wore feathers in their long, black, loose hair or tied to their weapons. None of their weapons appeared to be made of metal. All were either wood or stone. Their clothing, what they wore, was made from animal hides. Some were bare-chested in the morning chill. They wore paint on their chests like their faces.

We were larger, stronger and better equipped. While they fought with sticks and stones, we used strong, sharp, steel swords, heavy, broad-bladed battle axes, tough metal-clad shields, strong bows and metal-tipped arrows. Many of our men wore metal helmets and a few owned metal chest plates, though none had time to strap them on before the attack.

Leif shouted orders as the enemy got closer. "Hold firm men! Let the first wave attack, then take them down!"

Thirty or so men closed the gap between us and threw their weapons and themselves on our shields. Arrows from their rear stopped as they rushed to our line.

"Now!" Leif shouted. "Take them down!" We rose to our full height, pushing them off our shields. Most of us stood at least a head taller than our attackers. It appeared that they had never fought an enemy that used metal shields. Deflecting the strikes from their weapons with our shields was easy. Although they were fierce fighters, they were ineffective as we swung deadly bone-crunching blows, slicing through flesh with our battleaxes, heavy swords, and metal-spiked war clubs.

The skirmish lasted less than two minutes until Leif called us off. Many of the strange looking warriors were dead at our feet. Some that could get away on their own power did so. Others received help from their brothers as they carried or dragged them from the battle line.

Several of our men went after the stragglers as they limped away. "Leave them be," Leif ordered, calling them back. "You men," he pointed to about a dozen, "form a defensive archer line here. He drew a line in the sand with his bloody sword. "If any of the others have any fight left in them, take them out. Hold a line right here. The archers took a knee behind their shields, strung their arrows and waited. The surviving savages melted into the woods. No more arrows flew toward the Vikings that day.

"Load the boats, men, Leif said. "We'll find more hospitable shores to explore. While the boats were being loaded and readied to be launched, my father tended to my wound. Only four other men had injuries. I had almost forgotten about mine. It was nothing more than a deep scratch on my lower jaw. None of our men were killed.

My father examined my injury as he washed the blood off my face and neck. My thin beard was matted with blood. He grabbed my chin and looked at my face, twisting it one way and then the other in his hand. "That little scratch won't turn the girls away." He grinned. "You're still a handsome young man just like your father."

Soon both boats pulled away from the beach. Archers were positioned between each oarsman on the beach side, protecting our retreat from the beach, leaving our mysterious enemy to retrieve their dead, take care of their wounded, and wonder who those large warriors were that dealt them such a deadly blow.

After we were well into the bay, heading for open water, my rowing position was only a few feet from Leif at the tiller. I probably had the same things on my mind as the rest of the crew.

I asked the captain, "have you decided where we're going next?"

A smile crossed his face as he thought for a moment. "You don't think a couple of boatloads of Vikings are going to travel all this way through cold, deep water, survive a huge storm and a little scuffle with some wild people and just turn around and go home do you?"

"No sir, not if I know you like I think I do."

"You're right. We're Vikings. We're adventurers. There's a lot to explore. We have no idea how big this place is. We must learn what resources it has to offer.

"Holgar, we need to explore the coastline both south and north. We may spend several months here learning what this place has to offer. Winter will come soon. Perhaps we'll find a comfortable place to spend the winter, maybe we'll build a cabin for the men from some of these timbers that grow in such abundance here. We won't do the trip justice unless we trek overland to explore those areas also. Who knows, after we return home and tell of this place, some of our people may want to come here like our ancestors did in Iceland and Greenland. From what I've seen so far, this land may have much to offer."

I rowed with the men as we passed through the mouth of the bay into open water and turned south. Leif Ericson's Viking warriors had a long way to go and much to see.

My journey with them, however, ended there. I saw the tiny sparkles flash around me as I morphed out of Holgar's body.

The change didn't surprise me. I had become used to it as my way of traveling through time and jumping in and out of my host's bodies. I found it a thrilling and exciting way to start and finish my adventures. I watched the flashing images in time flicker before me. Each image moved forward in time—back to the present and to my bedroom.

CHAPTER 7

My night-time adventures never seemed to have any bearing on my getting a good night's rest. I stayed in bed for a while, listening to the morning sounds outside, thinking about my adventure with the Vikings. I brushed my finger against my jaw, reassuring myself that I could never be physically harmed, even though my host suffered an injury from the arrow to his jaw. What brave people they were; sailing off into the unknown, with no idea of what to expect and facing whatever dangers their voyage presented. I wondered if they ever dreamed of the potential the new land they discovered held. It would be eight-hundred years before some of their descendants would emigrate to the new world and settle in the Midwest.

Dad came home from work early. He got off work at noon. After lunch, we went to the garage to collect camping stuff and got it ready to pack in Mom's SUV.

While he tested a camping lantern, I asked, "Dad, how much do you know about the Vikings?"

"Vikings? You mean the pro football team?"

"No," I laughed. "The real Vikings from way back in history."

"Not much," he said, adjusting the intensity of the propane lantern. "Just what I've seen on The History Channel and from reading a few articles. Why?"

I hoisted the small propane bottle for the camp stove to see if I could tell how much propane was in the tank. "I got another book from Doctor Ma—I mean Grampa for reading over the summer. It's another book about history. This one is all about explorers.

"Last night I read an episode about how the Vikings sailed from Greenland and discovered America long before Columbus. I always thought Columbus discovered America. You know the rhyme, 'in 1492 Columbus sailed the ocean blue'. They taught us that in grade school."

"Max, the belief about Columbus was what most everybody held until researchers started turning up other information. I've seen a couple of programs about it on The History Channel. They found evidence that people they believed to be Vikings visited and explored North America hundreds of years before Columbus. Most of those findings happened just in the last hundred years or so. Archeologists found metal tools and other evidence that was dated from about four hundred years before Columbus made his famous voyages. They even found indications that shelters were made of logs where people stayed, perhaps over a winter or more as they explored their surroundings and took advantage of the resources they found. Of course, Native Americans didn't have metal tools then. They were still in the Stone Age. Some people even claim that strange markings found on rocks and stone walls as far west as the Great Lakes area and beyond were put there by Viking explorers."

"So," I said, putting the stove next to the lantern, "I wonder why they didn't move here then and create colonies like other Europeans would later?"

Dad pulled the tents from the garage cabinet. "I guess that's what makes history so interesting," he said. "Even after studying it as much as people do, there are still so many unanswered questions. It just makes you want to dig more to try to find answers to those questions."

He passed the tents off to me to stack by the car and reached for the sleeping bags. We had two extras from the time last year when Rick and Jeremy went camping with us. We pulled out an extra for Grampa and stacked them on the concrete next to the tents at the back of the car. Then we pulled the camp chairs out of storage and placed them beside the rest of the gear. I got the case of drinking water that Mom picked up at the market and put it with the stack of gear.

"What else?" I asked.

"We can't forget the fishing gear," Dad reached back into the closet.

"What have we forgotten?" I asked.

"Well, we each have our backpacks of clothes and personal items and, oh yeah, our box of important camping essentials." He retrieved a cardboard box from the closet, put it on the workbench and opened it. He touched each item as he called them out. "Four flashlights, two for each tent, extra batteries, two lighters, *and* a box of matches. There are also some newspapers for starting the fire, and two rolls of toilet paper—just in case the camp park restroom is out. Here's a hatchet, a camp saw, and a couple of bars of soap. We need to get some towels from the linen closet. I also put a coil of rope in there for whatever we may need."

He looked at the pile of gear on the floor next to the car. "I think that's about it for all the stuff we need to load. Let's go see if the girls have the camp kitchen ready to go.

Soon we had the entire back of the SUV stuffed with a large cooler and several canvas bags with food and kitchen stuff, five backpacks and all the gear that Dad and I took out of the garage storage cabinet, and were on the way to pick up Grampa.

Mom called him before we left home to tell him we were on the way. He must have been excited about going with us because he and his gear were waiting for us on the front porch when we pulled up.

He looked as excited as a little kid on Christmas morning to be going camping with us. After greetings and hugs, and getting his gear stowed in the crowded space at the back of the SUV, we were on our way to the state park and our long camping weekend. Dad offered Grampa the seat beside him in front, but he said he'd prefer to sit in the back between Megan and me. Mom sat next to Dad and listened to Megan and me talk to Grampa about the archeological digs that he'd worked on over the years.

We found an ideal campsite on an elevated spot overlooking the river with lots of trees for shade. It already had a picnic table next to a water faucet and the restrooms were within easy walking distance.

Dad is always particular about how the campsite is set up as to where the tents are in relation to the campfire, so it took a while to get things organized in a safe and orderly manner for the weekend.

While Dad and Grampa assembled the tents, and Mom and Megan arranged the lanterns and kitchen stuff the way they wanted them, I busied myself gathering firewood. I found several dead tree limbs had fallen to the ground in the woods. I brought them to our camp, and in a few minutes had them reduced to fire pit sized pieces.

It was still a couple of hours before sunset, so we decided to take a hike around the canyon rim to a nice lookout spot at the top of the canyon. The whole area was dotted with chalky limestone outcroppings and wooded with juniper and scrub oaks along the trail with occasional large, spreading live oak trees scattered about. Megan and I walked with Grampa while Mom and Dad followed. We walked for a while following a trail taking in the scenery. Then Grampa offered a suggestion. "You know the walk is fun and the scenery is great, but I think a game may make it even more interesting."

"We love games, Mom said. "What do you have in mind."

"Well, why don't we all try to find something that may be interesting to discuss as we walk along the trail. Maybe something that would be pretty ordinary until we take a moment to look closely at it to see what it really is. We can take turns finding things to point out to the others, and maybe see some things that we wouldn't otherwise see. I'll start first to give you an example."

He stopped on the trail, looking around at the ground. Then he stooped over and picked up what appeared to be an ordinary white, limestone rock.

"Here you go," he said as he rubbed the rock, removing some of the surface dirt and dust. He held it out for us to look. "What do you see?"

"There are little ridges on it," Megan said, taking it in her hand and running her fingers over the rock. She handed it off to the rest of us.

"It's a fossil," Grampa said. "It's the fossil of a sea creature that lived millions of years ago. They're all over the place."

"A sea creature?" Megan exclaimed. "How'd it get way up here? We're halfway up the hillside."

"Well," Grampa smiled, "at one time, this whole part of the country was a shallow sea, all covered in water. The small sea creatures lived out their life cycle and died, forming many layers along with the undersea silt. That's what made this limestone we're standing on. It was the sea bottom. Then over millions of years, the shallow seas dried up and the earth's crust started moving. Some parts moved against other parts very slowly, but with great force." He made fists of his hands and pushed them together showing how the parts of the earth pushed against each other. "This caused many parts of the earth to be pushed upward, sometimes many thousands of feet. That's what caused the mountains to be formed." He illustrated by moving his fists upward.

"So now, millions of years later, that little fossil that once lived as a sea creature is now up on a mountainside."

"Wow, that's a cool story," Megan said. "Can I keep the fossil?"

"Sure, but if you look closely, you may see more; maybe even more striking than that one. So, who's next to find something beyond the ordinary right here in plain sight?"

"I think I found something," Dad said. "Look over here."

He was pointing about six feet off the trail to the trunk of a live oak tree. "Come over here and check this out."

We gathered around the tree to see what had caught his attention. About a foot and a half off the ground, a tuft of grayish hair was caught in the bark of the tree.

"What do you think that came from?" Mom asked.

"Don't know," Dad said, reaching to pull a few strands from the tuft. "Let's try to figure this out." He examined the hairs and passed them around as we mentioned the different animals that could have left part of its fur attached to the tree.

"Maybe it was a raccoon, Megan said.

"I don't think so," Dad said. A raccoon isn't that tall if he was just passing by."

"But what if he was climbing the tree?"

"Yeah, good point, but I don't think the hair color is right for a raccoon."

We named off several other animals including possum, skunk, fox and even mountain lion, and discounted all of them because of hair color difference from the sample we were studying.

"How about a coyote or a wolf," Mom said.

"Hmm," Dad said. Maybe you have something there. I don't think there are any wolves in this part of the country anymore. Haven't been for years. But there are coyotes. Mama, I think you've solved this puzzle. Let's call it a coyote, roaming around looking for a meal."

We could have made it to the top of the ridge in less than twenty minutes from where we were, but we spent the next hour taking our time, stopping every few minutes to explore nature, and look—really look at the little details around us. We compared the veins in different kinds leaves, and noted the color changes of the layers of the rock formations on the canyon wall across from us. We noticed how the juniper tree's roots clung to the cracks in the edge of the canyon wall. We stopped for a few minutes to drink water and identify shapes in the slowly moving clouds overhead.

Finally, we made it to the top of the ridge and sat on a rock outcropping looking at the fantastic panoramic view of the rolling hills that ultimately stretched out to a flatland prairie. The sun was still a little above the horizon, and the fluffy, white clouds we had identified shapes in a few minutes earlier had given way to a layer of high, wispy clouds that captured the sun's rays presenting a magnificent evening light show of yellows, pinks, oranges, reds, and purples.

"What a great view," Grampa said.

The reds and oranges of the western sky reflected off our faces while we enjoyed the next few minutes of the brilliant colors changing as the sun dropped slowly beyond the horizon. The majesty of the moment silenced us for some time while the stunning show played out.

When the bright colors were replaced by less exciting hues, Dad said, "Hey guys, it's gonna be dark soon. We'd better get back down to camp."

Luckily, I had stowed my flashlight in my lightweight backpack, because it was fully dark before we got back to camp.

It was no trouble getting the camp ready for the evening, because of the work we did before our hike. In a few minutes, the camp was well lit with two lanterns, and we all pitched in to make dinner.

"I didn't think you'd mind a simple meal of sandwiches and chips tonight," Mom said. "There's some potato salad too. I also have the makings for smores later around the fire." Megan and I grinned at the mention of smores. That was one of our favorite things to do while camping.

We enjoyed our meal around the picnic table with lively conversation about our hike and fishing plans for the next day.

"I got a new fishing tip the other day," I said.

What's that?" Dad said.

"Well," I grinned, "according to Boomer, Jeremy's little brother, spitting on your bait brings in the big ones. He said that was his grampa's fishing recipe." I turned to my grandfather. "Do you have any sure-fire fishing recipes?"

"No, afraid not. Guess I was too busy chasing other interest rather than fishing when I was younger. But I'm anxious to learn. Maybe you can share some of your fishing secrets with me."

"Be glad to," I said. "But mostly all we do is just drown worms."

CHAPTER 8

After dinner, we gathered our camp chairs around the fire while Mom brought out the smores stuff. Dad and Grampa cut some thin, green twigs from a willow tree and prepared them to roast marshmallows over the fire a little later.

Most of the conversation around the fire was directed at our new grandfather. There was still so much we all wanted to know about him.

Megan seemed to be the most inquisitive. She asked, "You must have changed your name when you left Europe, right? It hasn't always been Magas, has it?"

"Oh no, I changed it many years ago, when I left the old country. My birth name was just too difficult to pronounce for most people."

"So why did you decide to use 'Magas' as your name?" she asked. "We know that means magic."

Doctor Magas hesitated a long moment, lowered his chin to his chest, and took a long sigh before looking up and answering. "Ever since I met you all, I knew the time would come when we would need to have this discussion. I guess this is it.

"You see, magic has always been a part of who I am." He looked around at each of us. "I learned as a very young person that I had a special gift." He looked down for a moment, gathering his thoughts, then looked back at us. The firelight glistened in his eyes as he told his story.

"That gift is a certain kind of power; or special ability that comes with being a part of this family. It's always been with us. Some of our clan, hundreds of years ago, were mystics. Some were wizards and some were brilliant scientists. But most were just regular people without any apparent supernatural talent. It's a very rare condition that not all family members have. Most have traces of it, but not enough to amount to anything. Some have had the power, but didn't know what to do with it. It frightened many to the point that they concealed and never sought to develop it.

"In the last hundred years or so there's only been a handful like myself that worked and practiced to develop and harness these powers. I've used it to assist in my work as a historian and an archeologist. There is one thing I've been very cautious about—I've always been very vigilant to use my special ability for the betterment and enlightenment of man."

Megan, Mom, and Dad were dumbfounded. They were speechless until Megan blurted out, "That means that Mom, Max and I could all have special—magical—powers?"

His gaze again moved between the three of us. "Yes," he said calmly, it's *a fact* that all of you three have very special powers."

"Now, I don't want to burst anybody's bubble," Dad said in his level-headed, 'let's check out all the facts' way. "You're saying this is *real* magic, not just some parlor game of 'pull the flower bouquet out of your sleeve' magic to entertain friends at a party type of thing, right?"

"That's right."

Dad continued, "I assume there are different types of magic. So, what kind of magic do you do? Do you do things like put spells and hexes on people?"

"No, nothing like that. Those things can be dangerous. Most of what I'm involved with has to do with movement and transport."

"I don't mean to offend you, and I hope you understand," Dad said, "but I like to see what someone's claiming they can do, rather than just accept what they say."

Mom cut her eyes at Dad in a disapproving way but said nothing.

"Oh, no offense is taken at all," Grampa said smiling. "In fact, I expected you to be skeptical of what I just told you. I'll be happy to give you a demonstration, but first I need to ask you something very important."

"What's that?" Dad asked.

"Well, as you may or may not have noticed, I'm not the kind of man that seeks attention. I've lived a rather quiet life and have been lucky enough to have found a certain level of success through discovery in my fields. It's happened without any fanfare. That's the way I like it. I've made sure that there haven't been major press releases about the important archeological finds my team has made over the years, and the historical books I've written, although rather scholarly, haven't been presented to the world as publishing release event, even though they are widely read in historical circles and required reading in many universities. But the areas of my life that remain absolutely secret to the world are the special powers that I use in my work and on a personal level. No one, but a very trusted few, know of these powers.

"So, you—my family," his intense gaze darted between me, Megan and Mom, "like it or not, also possess those powers.

"Sorry Tom, this doesn't apply you because you and I aren't blood relatives. But I hope you'll be supportive of what I'm telling them.

Looking back at Mom, Megan and me, Grampa said, "Those powers lie latent within you, like a spark waiting to be kindled and brought to full flame. I owe it to you to expose and explain them, so you'll know what power you have. You can then decide what, if anything, you'll do with it.

"As you can imagine, if this knowledge of your ability should fall into the wrong hands, it could become at the least, awkward and difficult for you, and at the worst, actually dangerous for you. So, I must ask that you respect the secrecy of the power and reveal it only to your spouse and offspring when they are old enough to understand. No one else should ever know of the power. Can I have the pledge of secrecy from each of you?"

I spoke up first. "You've got it from me for sure!"

Megan echoed my pledge. "I agree too."

Mom responded, "Now I'm beginning to see the possible source of some of the things about me that I've never been able to put my finger on. I've always called it my sixth sense. Some things I just know without knowing why I know it. Like when I knew that Megan had that fender bender when she first started driving. I knew about it before she even called me to tell me it happened.

That's not the only time things like that have happened to me. Yes, you've got my pledge and I definitely want to know more."

Dad tugged at his ear like he does sometimes when he's making a tough decision. "I'm not inheriting anything from you except what I'll learn from you as a friend and family member because I believe you to be a wise man. So, I'm giving you the acceptance of what you say, as you prove your abilities. I also pledge to your request for secrecy."

Grampa's beard spread in a smile as big as I'd ever seen. "Thank you all for your trust. I know you won't regret it. Now, I have something for each of you that I'd like to deliver in a special way. Let's all stand, if you would, and circle the fire."

He pushed himself from his camp chair while each of us did the same, and circled ourselves with equal spacing around the fire. He reached into his pants pocket and produced a small, red velvet bag that was closed with a string tie at the top. He loosened the tie and reached inside to withdraw a handful of small items that were wrapped in white tissue paper. He partially removed the paper on a couple of the items until he selected one and removed the paper completely. The flickering light from the fire glistened off a golden, signet ring. He held it out in front of his chest in his fingers and faced Mom, who was directly across the fire from him, about seven feet away.

"Susan," he said, looking her in the eyes, "position your right hand in front of your body with your palm toward the ground and your fingers outstretched toward me." She did what he said.

He slowly opened his fingers allowing the golden ring to settle into the palm of his hand. He focused his eyes on the ring. Its gold glistened from the firelight as it slowly lifted from his hand and floated—suspended in the air, slowly making its way over the flames and eased itself onto Mom's ring finger on her right hand.

I didn't know how he did it, but somehow, he effortlessly guided the ring through the air with just the power in his eyes and his mind.

Mom's chin dropped and her eyes widened as the ring floated over the flames and onto her hand. She was speechless.

"Susan, my dear, please accept this ring with my love to my daughter. The emblem on your ring is the family crest that my ancestors wore when they were in the court of kings, centuries ago. I have renamed the crest as now being from *The House of Discovery*, as that is what we now do. We seek information. We discover, and we try to better the world with our discoveries."

"Oh. My. Goodness!" Mom managed to whisper as she fingered the shiny, new ring. "I can't believe what I just saw."

"Believe it," Grampa said smiling and turned to Megan. "Megan, now it's your turn. Extend your hand like your mother did."

He removed the tissue wrapping from another ring and repeated the process. He ignored Megan's giggling as he continued to focus his energy on the ring passing gently through the air and onto her finger. "Wow! That's so cool! Can you teach me to do that?"

"There's much that you can learn, but all in due time, my dear. Megan, please accept this ring with my love to my beautiful granddaughter. Know that your future is wide open to you. You can, and will with appropriate effort, accomplish whatever you set your mind to do."

Then he turned to me. "Now for the birthday boy," His eyes twinkled in the firelight as he smiled at me. "You didn't think I'd forget about your birthday, did you? Max, lift your hand like your mother and sister did."

He unwrapped another gold ring. This one was larger than the other two. He held it momentarily between his fingers before he sent it slowly through the air to nestle on my finger. It was as if he controlled a magical, invisible beam that caused it to levitate and float to me. When it settled on my finger, it had a warm, comfortable feeling. It felt really good on my hand.

"Thank you," I said quietly. I was deeply moved by the gesture he was making to our family.

"Max," he said, looking at me with the glow of a proud grandfather. "You are such a very special young man. I want to thank you for being the conduit that linked me with the rest of my family. As I've gotten to know you over the last couple of months, I've found you to be everything I'd hoped a grandson would be. You're so intelligent and open to whatever challenge comes your way. I know you too will have a wonderful future."

Then he turned to Dad. "Tom, even though I knew you would be skeptical of me and the paranormal things I do, I also have a ring for you." He unwrapped the tissue paper from the last ring. "Show me your finger." Again, he sent the ring through the air, over the fire, and onto Dad's finger.

"That's amazing!" Dad said in awe. "Forget everything I said about real magic. I just saw something impossible happen. So, I'm believing everything you say—no questions asked."

"Thank you for your new-found confidence in me. I appreciate it. And thank you for allowing me to assume my place in this family.

"Now with all of us wearing the same ring," he showed us that the ring he wore was identical to ours, "we have a physical bond that also holds us together.

"You all should know that every part of your ring holds a special meaning." He removed his ring from his hand and examined it as he described the different parts.

"The circular shape of your ring represents the never-ending circle of life. You, wearing the ring and being the center of that circle, carry the responsibility to make your life something of which you will be proud. It's up to you to leave this world a better place because you were here. Don't ever just take from your world, give back whatever you can.

"The largest part of the ring's face is a battle shield. The shield represents the strength of your body and mind to resist negative influences that may try to overcome your defenses and make you a weaker person.

"The helmet above the shield with the visor opened represents your open-mindedness. You are willing to accept new and different thoughts and information, but you also have a filter that can be used to evaluate, examine, and perhaps discard negative thoughts or information that may try to work its way into your mind.

"The vision ports of the helmet are always open symbolizing your vigilance to stay alert to the activities around you; to be able to react to any threat as it happens. The full visibility also allows you the ability to make good decisions before an event becomes an emergency.

"The crossed swords over the shield represent your willingness to use whatever means necessary to protect not only your family, but your beliefs, and your way of life.

"And finally, the feathered plumes leaning on either side of the helmet represent you as a scholar to not only seek truth but also document what you learn for the betterment of mankind.

"If you should ever start questioning your motives, or your direction in life, just take a moment to reflect on the values that are symbolized by the ring you wear. Those characteristics will serve you well."

I traced my fingernail along each part of the ring's face as he explained its meaning and realized that the ring was what he was working on the day I visited him in his studio. The fact that he created that ring for me with his own hands made it that much more special. I will wear it always.

We all stood looking at our rings as he finished describing the symbolism of its parts. It was quiet around the campfire with only the crackling of the burning log to break the silence for a few moments until Grampa spoke again.

"What you've just experienced is only a miniscule part of the power we share. The power within you may be limitless. It's up to you to develop it. I'll be exposing you to other facets of your ability in time—if you wish. I think we've covered enough for tonight.

"Now," he said with a smile inching across his face, "since we have that behind us, isn't it time for smores?"

We not only made smores over the fire that night, but Mom had somehow smuggled a birthday cake and candles into the car for the trip to the campsite and hidden it in her tent. My fifteenth birthday was one I would never forget.

The rest of the weekend was filled with fishing, swimming, hiking and hanging around the camp to rest between other activities. Nights were fun around the campfire because of Grampa amusing us with some of his levitating skills. He made us all; Mom, Megan and I realize that we did indeed have his special power by showing us how to focus on objects to actually make them move.

Before we knew it, our time on the river was gone and the camping weekend was over.

Although we were all tired from a busy weekend full of physical activities, the drive home was punctuated with laughter and talk of plans for future events we'd all do together.

When we pulled up at Grampa's house, we all got out to get his gear and give him a hug.

"Papa," Mom said as she held his hands after their embrace, "This is one of the best weekends of my entire life, getting to know you the way we did. We had a great time. We're so glad you were with us."

"Thank you for having me. It was a very special time for me," he said, reaching for his bag that I'd retrieved from the back of the car. I put his other gear on the porch and started to get back in the car. Grampa put his arm around my shoulder and said, "Thank you so much for bringing us all together. This couldn't have happened without you."

"I'm just glad it worked out this way," I said. "I never had a Grampa before." I slid in the backseat of the car as he held the door open for me.

He closed the car door and waved as we pulled out of his driveway and headed home.

CHAPTER 9

I passed my hand over the leather cover of the big book that night as I got ready for bed. I felt a tiny tingle as my fingers lingered on the book's cover. It's hard to explain the feeling I got. It's almost like it was a power reaching out to make a connection with me. It didn't shock or sting me. It didn't hurt at all. It was just a comfortable, warm feeling.

The anticipation of my next adventure got the best of me. I crawled into bed to my normal reading position, on my belly. I pulled the big book into the bed with me and turned to the next chapter, *The Corps of Discovery Expedition*. I carefully stretched the leather book marker into the spine and started reading.

The Lewis and Clark Expedition, 1804 – 1806

The Lewis and Clark expedition, sponsored by President Thomas Jefferson and the United States Government was the first American expedition to cross and explore the newly acquired territories of the western United States.

Just a year earlier, in April, 1803 a treaty was signed between the United States government and France transferring ownership of a huge amount of land in the western part of the U.S. from France to America.

Two army officers, Captain Meriwether Lewis and Lieutenant William Clark, were handpicked by President Jefferson to lead a group of about thirty men on what became more than a two-year expedition through all kinds of terrain and weather. They were charged with not only mapping the area and finding a waterway to the Pacific but were also expected to prepare extensive reports on previously unknown plants, animals, and the native inhabitants.

On May 14, 1804, the Corps of Discovery shoved their keelboats into the Missouri River at the frontier outpost called Camp Dubois and headed upstream marking the beginning of their voyage to the Pacific coast. It would be another two years, four months, and ten days before they would once again return to civilization.

Just as I was looking forward to getting into the Lewis and Clark story, the now familiar tiny spark-like fairy dust surged upward from the leather bookmarker to twinkle all around me. Within seconds, my aura left my physical body on the bed and hovered a few moments over it before transporting me into the past.

As always, the flashes of historical scenes regressing into the past fascinated me. Then the changing scenes slowed and stopped as I felt the changes occur in me. I was body-jumping into my next host. After as many time-travel adventures as I had taken, I was accustomed to the transition process and felt comfortable with it. But I never knew exactly what the circumstances would be when I joined my new host. I expected that if it was like most transitions, I would find myself in the middle of something exciting. I wasn't disappointed.

"Ah-han-ne-ani-ci-sne-kte-nil," the wrinkled old man chanted with other words whose meanings were lost to me as he knelt on both knees and leaned over the semi-conscious boy. From time to time he held a rattlesnake's rattle over the boy's head and shook it as he repeated his chants. Frequently, he picked up the clay bowl that held a wad of smoldering herbs and gently blew the smoke over the boy's body.

The ancient looking medicine man wore leather clothing like most of the others in the teepee. The old woman with the blanket draped over her shoulders waited at the edge of the firelight's glow on her knees, several feet away from the almost lifeless eight-year-old boy, waiting to assist the old man with whatever he needed.

My attention hung on every move and incantation the old man uttered, and how he used the medicine his woman concocted for him. While he worked over the boy, I also took inventory of who, when and where I was.

I had jumped into the body and became a part of Jake McAllister, a nineteen-year-old soldier, adventurer and budding naturalist with the Lewis and Clark Expedition of 1804. I was in an Indian lodge watching the old medicine man perform his healing ritual over a very sick young boy.

One of Captain Lewis primary obligations on his expedition, as defined by President Thomas Jefferson, was to collect and document native plants and animals that were unknown in the eastern part of North America, and develop relationships with the native people if possible.

I volunteered at every opportunity to accompany Captain Lewis with a small group of hunters on his nature walks alongside the river to collect specimens as the rest of the company rowed our small flotilla upstream. Sometimes those excursions lasted several days before we reunited with the rest of the corps back at the river. The captain soon realized that he and I shared a keen interest in the plants and wildlife we encountered, and I maintained good records.

Over time, he came to consider me his unofficial assistant in the collection, preservation, and documentation of specimens we found along the way. I also kept a double set of technical journals about our findings; one for Captain Lewis, and one for me. We kept them in separate locations at camp and on the move for safety purposes. The last thing we wanted to do was to lose any of that important information.

As winter approached, after months of rowing our keelboats up-river, drawing maps, and gathering specimens, we met and became friendly with a large village of Mandan Indians. We built our winter quarters, a log fort we called Fort Mandan, across the upper Missouri River from the Indian village. They were a peaceful tribe that lived in log and mud lodges.

We would have had a difficult time surviving the harsh winter and deep snows without their help. The long winter brought extremely cold temperature, strong winds, and driving snow. Many from our company hunted with the Mandans to find the scarce game that winter. The Indians frequently gifted us other food when hunting failed or the winter weather kept us from venturing out to hunt. We were thankful for their friendship. After our winter quarters were completed, some of us spent many cold afternoons and evenings with them, learning their ways.

My interest in learning about and using the native plants as medicine drew me to the tribe's respected elder and medicine man, they called Hota Ohanzee, or Strong Shadow. After developing a friendship with him and gaining his trust, he indulged me by using sign language and an interpreter we had with the crew to show and explain uses of his collection of medicinal plants. As I slowly gained a limited understanding of their language, I learned of the healing powers of some special barks, roots, and leaves from that region.

He also allowed me to watch some of his healing rituals. During that winter, I saw him successfully treat everything from toothaches and belly aches to broken bones. But the young Indian boy that was brought to his lodge that cold, snowy day appeared to be on the edge of death with a fever. It would take everything Strong Shadow had to pull him through.

The boy was semi-conscious. His skin was hot and he didn't respond to anyone. Several elders and the boy's parents were allowed to enter the healer's lodge and sit in the shadows to observe. I felt honored to be allowed to watch as he worked his medicine on the boy.

I sat on the opposite side of the lodge from the tribe elders, next to a stack of hides and extra buffalo robes. Among the elders was a drummer waiting for the old man to commence his healing ritual.

The old man spent a good while positioning his patient next to the fire and organizing his small bags of medicines. He was assisted by his main wife, an old woman herself. She said nothing as she helped him sort and lay out the small leather bags in neat rows on a soft, tanned deer hide. Once he was satisfied that everything he needed was close by and ready, he and the old woman knelt beside the boy and he started his chant.

"Ah-han-ne-ani-ci-sne-kte-nil," he wailed in his high pitched, reedy voice. He repeated that phrase several times. I recognized those words to mean "get well". He then launched into other words and phrases I only partially understood. He was imploring that the Great Spirit hear his plea to help heal the boy.

The old drummer joined him with a soft but steady drumbeat. The chanting continued as he lit some plant material in a small, clay bowl. It started to smolder, giving off a pungent smell. He blew on it, increasing the volume of smoke wafting from the bowl, then fanned it using an eagle feather fan, sending smoke over the small body lying on the robe next to the fire. He alternated between fanning the smoke over the boy, shaking the rattle, and rubbing the boy's head, face and chest with his hands while varying the volume of the chants.

Every once in a while, the old man stopped chanting long enough to utter instructions to the old woman. She selected one of the little medicine bags and poured a small amount of the ground-up material into one of the clay bowls of water at the edge of the fire. After letting it boil for a few minutes, she removed it from the fire, stirred it carefully to allow the active ingredients to become one with the water and blew on it to cool, then handed it to the old man. He then made the semi-conscious boy drink. He repeated this process several times with concoctions from different bags. Each time as he poured the liquid down the boy's throat, he increased the volume of his chanting. When she handed him the

91

fourth cup, he took it into his own mouth, swished it around, pulled the buffalo hide away from the boy and spat the dark liquid onto the boy's body. He spat several times; each with a big gush of breath, splattering it all over the youngster's body.

The old man had worked up a heavy sweat, even though it was extremely cold outside with deep snow on the ground. With the boy still uncovered, the healer wiped sweat from his face and smeared it, along with the medicine he spat, over the little boy. He then covered him again with the warm buffalo robe.

The drummer continued his steady beat through the entire process, only varying the volume and intensity to coincide with the chanting of the medicine man.

Strong Shadow then stood—never stopping his chanting, and motioned to the old woman to move his medicines out of his way. He began a shuffling kind of dance around the fire next to the boy, shaking the snake rattle over the boy's body. I was amazed that over an hour of the intense ritual of chanting to the drumbeat, using herbal smoke, giving multiple doses of healing medicines, the laying of hands, and shaking the rattle the way he did that he still had strength left to do a ritual dance. He made several circuits around the boy with his slow, measured gait following the steady, rhythmic beat of the drummer. On his third pass around the boy, he reached into a bag, pulled out a small handful of something and threw it into the fire, causing it to flash momentary, lighting even the far corners of the lodge for a second or two. The moment the flash occurred, the drumming, dancing and chanting abruptly stopped. The sudden silence inside the lodge took me by surprise.

The boy's eyes fluttered open. After a moment, they managed to focus on his mother and he slowly reached his hand toward her. Several of the elders silently nodded their approval as the mother rushed to her son.

Strong Shadow, exhausted from his physical efforts and calling upon the Spirits to help heal the boy, almost collapsed at my feet. I put a soft bear rug under him to recline after such an energy-sapping ritual.

His woman produced a ceremonial smoking pipe with a long stem adorned with feathers and paint. She had already loaded it with trade tobacco and touched it off with a small flaming stick from the fire. She drew on it several times to assure it was well lit then handed it to her husband.

I had picked up enough sign language and Mandan words by that time to engage in minimal, simple conversation.

"Very good," I said smiling as I patted him on the back.

"Um, yes. Very good." He responded after taking a long draw on his pipe and offering it to me.

That winter was cold, damp, dark and just plain miserable except for the time I spent at the Mandan village. I did my part gathering firewood for our camp, which we needed plenty for those long, cold nights. I also spent many days with hunting parties, seeking out and following animal tracks to bring meat, any kind of meat, back to camp. But I looked forward to spending as much of my spare time as I could over the remainder of the winter with Strong Shadow learning of his medicines and treatment techniques, and documenting everything I'd learned in my journals.

He seemed to enjoy having a student to teach. He explained, as well as our language barriers allowed, the ailment each type of medicine was used for and how they were prepared. Each day I spent learning from him, I became more excited about the potential of unlocking cures from using components of natural growing things. I'd seen first-hand what they could do. I knew that finding those cures was an adventure I wanted to be a part of.

Unfortunately, I wasn't able to obtain the most important information—where he found them, and what they looked like in their original, living form because of the weather and the time of year. I'd have to be in the area during the other seasons to see first-hand how he found and collected his medicine chest. He did, however, give me some information that I believed would be helpful in my further travels.

"Some medicines come from far away," he said, pointing and looking off into the distance as if he was looking at a far corner of the world. "Many moons travel. Far, far away."

My journey back in time to the Lewis and Clark Expedition ended late that night after I dutifully documented my visit with Strong Shadow.

As Jake drifted off to sleep in his straw-stuffed bunk, I saw the tiny sparkles flash around me and the fine dust-like particles encircled me while my vapor morphed out of Jake's body and floated away.

The next I knew; I was waking up to a new day in my bedroom. I stretched my body, feeling refreshed and rested. But something nagged at me from my last journey. With the Lewis and Clark expedition lasting almost two and a half years and covering thousands of miles in such a monumental adventure, why was my visit so short and focused primarily on the old Mandan medicine man during the first winter on the trip? There were so many more thrilling things to experience. Doctor Magas controlled the destination and duration of each of my adventures, so I needed to get those answers from him. But there was one thing that I was sure of; young Jake McAllister' interest in natural healing was sparked, and he got a good, basic understanding of Native American cures during that winter of 1805.

CHAPTER 10

I'd like to review my latest adventure with my grandfather and get his feedback, but I also felt a need to spend some time with my friends. I certainly didn't want to get out of touch with them while I was chasing adventure with my secret time travels.

I called the guys after breakfast and made plans to get together for a bike ride down to the city park for a dip in the pool. Jeremy and I met at Rick's house and we took off from there for the ten-minute ride to the park. Traffic was light and the summer temperature was already pushing the low nineties at mid-morning on the tree-lined residential streets. We kept an eye out for traffic as we rode three abreast so we could talk. We chatted about nothing in particular until Rick asked out of the blue,

"So, what do you guys think you want to do when you get all grown up and out of school?"

Jeremy and I looked at each other wondering where that question came from, but that was Rick. We both thought a minute and Jeremy answered first.

"Well, you know my mom's a nurse. She's always made it pretty clear that she'd like to see me to do something in the medical field."

"You mean like a doctor? Rick asked.

"She would like that, but I don't think it would be for me," Jeremy said shrugging. "There's all kind of things you can do in the medical field from medical research to running a doctor's office. And I'm okay with that. How about you, Rick?"

"You know, I've been thinking about that," he said. "It's never too early to start thinking about what you want to do with your life. I've thought about being either a brain surgeon or an astronaut. Brain surgeons make lots of money and astronauts get lots of glory. That sounds pretty cool to me. Or maybe a cowboy. Now that would be a fun job. How about you, Max?"

I looked at Rick for a long take before I answered. "You know, all along, I always thought I'd like to be an engineer. I like to tinker with things and solve problems. That's kinda what a lot of engineers do. But lately, I've been drawn to something involved with history and archeology."

"You mean you want to teach history?"

"Well, maybe I could teach, but I could really see myself doing something a bit different. Something like historical and archeological research. That's what my grampa does. He doesn't find it boring at all, In fact, it's pretty exciting."

"What grampa? Rick said. "You've never mentioned a grampa before. Where does he live?"

"Right here in town."

"Since when?"

"It's kind of a long story. We just recently learned about him. He's been looking for us for a long time. So now we have a grampa and he's a pretty cool dude." I smiled, realizing for the first time that I really did indeed have a cool dude for a grampa.

We enjoyed the pool for about an hour. By then it was approaching lunch time. We had planned to have a burger for lunch downtown. We decided after we changed clothes at the pool to head to the town square for a burger basket.

"Hey," Rick said, "where does this new grampa of yours live?"

"He lives right off the square, downtown. Why"

"I thought you may want him to join us for lunch." Rick grinned. "I've never met a cool grampa. Most old people I know are kinda boring and old-fashioned. Some are even grumpy. Do you have his number?"

"Yeah."

"Go on, then. Give him a call."

"Naah, he may be busy," I said, shaking my head. "I kinda hate to bother him on such short notice."

"Aw, come on, Max." Jeremy joined in. "I bet he'd like to know your friends. All grandparents want to know their grandkids don't run around with a bunch of hoodlums.

"Oh, you mean we're not hoodlums?" Rick joked. "That's good to know."

I rolled my eyes, reached for my cell phone and punched in Grampa's number. After two rings, I heard Jeffery's deep bass voice with the Caribbean accent.

"Magas residence."

"Hi, Jeffery. This is Max. Is my grandfather there?"

"As a matter of fact, he's right here next to me."

I could hear the smile in his voice come through the phone.

"Just a moment," he said. "I'll put him on."

"Within seconds, I heard the slight European accent of my grandfather's voice.

"Hello, Max. What a nice surprise. How are you?"

"Oh, I'm fine. Hey, I'm hanging out with a couple of my friends, Rick and Jeremy. We've been swimming down at the park and were thinking about having a burger on the square and thought you may like to join us. I'd like for you to meet the guys."

"I'd really love to meet your friends. As a matter of fact, Jeffery and I were just talking about lunch. It seems that he's serving a dish today that we haven't had in a while. He just got back from the market a few minutes ago. Hang on just a minute, Max. I'll be right back."

"Okay." I heard muffled voices on the phone for a few moments before he came back on the line.

"You know, Max, the thought of a juicy burger downtown sounds really good, but since you'll be so close to my place when you're downtown, we'd like for you to come over here and join us for lunch. Jeffery seems to think you and your friends will enjoy what he has on the menu."

My face lit up. "You know I will! Let me see what they say." I held my finger over the microphone hole on the phone and checked with the guys. Returning to the phone, I said, "When do you want us there?"

"Whenever you get here will be fine. Jeffery said he may just include three hungry teenagers as his kitchen staff."

"It won't take us more than a few minutes to get there," I told him.

"Wow! Your grampa lives here?" Rick said as we pulled into the large covered parking space next to the house. "He must be really rich." He and Jeremy were checking out the beautiful gardens and the impeccably remodeled Victorian-style house.

"I don't know about that, but he likes nice things," I said. I led them up the wide staircase onto the porch and to the large, stained-glass front door.

Grampa answered the doorbell himself. "Well, hello boys," he said with a smile. "Come on in." After I made the introductions, including Jeffery who was behind the kitchen island bar, Grampa led us around to the backside of the island. Jeffery was in the process of laying out things from his pantry, refrigerator and grocery bags for a good, healthy lunch. When he had all kinds of fruit, vegetables, and some fish organized on the counter, he asked, "Is anybody hungry?"

"I don't know about the rest of them, but I sure am," Rick said grinning. "What can we do to help?"

"The first thing, we'll all do is wash our hands," Jeffery said as he squirted liquid soap in each of our palms.

Within minutes we were all elbow deep in putting lunch together. Jeremy sliced strawberries, cherries, and bananas for a fruit dip appetizer while Rick and Grampa worked on a batch of banana-berry smoothies. Jeffery took care of the fish taco preparation and got the fish in the oven while I made the mango salsa for the tacos. After I got the salsa made and set aside, I shifted over to give Jeremy a hand with the cream cheese recipe for the fruit dip. While we were putting things together, Rick commented about how much we were making.

"Wow," he said, "looks like we're making enough to feed twice as many as we have here."

"Oh, trust me," Jeffery said, "it won't go to waste. Just before Jeffery served everything up, he reached for the walkie-talkie on his belt and spoke into it.

"Three to control."

After a moment, a man's voice spoke through the hand-held device. "This is control."

"Lunch is ready," Jeffery said as he dished the food up into two different sets of serving dishes.

"Who was that?" The always curious Rick asked.

I looked at Grampa for his answer.

"That was Mister Hatcher." We call him Hatch. He's doing some work for me."

"Oh yeah? What kind of work?"

Rick was a good kid, but a little lacking in social graces. Sometimes you just don't dig into what people do unless the information is offered. I waited to see how Grampa would answer that.

"Well, Mister Hatcher does several things for me. He's the landscape designer and maintains the gardens, and he also helps me do some historical research. Sometimes I write books based on our research."

"Wow! That's cool. Max didn't say you were a writer. Maybe I've read one. 'Course I don't read too much, just textbooks for school when I have to."

"Perhaps you'll read one of mine when you get in college. Some universities use them as history texts." Grampa said. "Max is reading one of my books now about American adventurers.

Their conversation was interrupted when Hatch turned the corner into the kitchen pushing an empty cart. After introductions were made, Jeffery helped Hatch load the cart with serving dishes and he headed back the way he came.

We then sat down to what Jeffery called his Summer Fish Taco Razzle Dazzle Fruit Lunch.

"I'm glad Max brought you by today," Grampa said to Rick and Jeremy. "I can imagine your summer without school is keeping you busy. I know Max was ready for summer vacation. What do you do to fill up your days?"

"What don't we do," Rick said. "Let's see. There's fishing, swimming, baseball, basketball, bike riding, camping, stock car racing, skateboarding, and of course, chores. We all do lots of chores, right guys?"

Jeremy and I both knew he was blowing smoke about chores, but we let it ride. Before we knew it, almost an hour had passed while we enjoyed Jeffery's lunch and listened to Rick explain his new skate board ramp in his backyard.

Grampa noted that we all cleaned our plates. "Sure glad you guys weren't very hungry," he joked. "There's more if you want it."

Rick smiled and rolled his eyes while Jeremy shook his head and rubbed his stomach, indicating they'd had more than enough. "No, thank you sir," I said. "That was really good."

"How about a little tour of the shop and studio in the backyard while your food settles?" Grampa said.

"Thanks, but we'd better let you and Jeffery get back to work," I said.

"Maybe next time we'll plan for you all to help me make something in the shop," Grampa said as he ushered us to the door.

"Max," he called from the porch as we walked to our bicycles, call me tonight. I'd like to know what you thought about that last chapter you read."

"I'll do that," I said, waving as we rolled into the street and headed home.

That evening after a nice dinner with good family conversation, I excused myself early after kitchen cleanup and went to my room to make my call to Grampa and read. He answered on the second ring.

"Hello Max," he said.

"Hey, I wanted to let you know before I forgot, just how much we enjoyed the lunch today. Be sure and tell Jeffery."

"I appreciate that, and I'm sure Jeffery will be pleased. I'll pass the word."

"We finished dinner a little while ago and I'm up in my room. I hope I didn't interrupt your dinner or anything," I asked.

"No, we won't have dinner for another hour. So, tell me, Max, how did your last adventure go?"

"I found it to be really educational. Maybe more educational than adventurous. I learned a lot for sure."

"Like what?"

"Well, for one thing, Jake McAllister got a good understanding of natural cures from an Indian medicine man. Yeah, this old Indian guy taught him lots of stuff about medicine he made from plants."

"Did McAllister document what he learned from the medicine man?"

"You bet he did. He wrote everything down about all the plants and barks and roots the old man used. The old man can cure all kinds of stuff using his little bags of ground-up plants and roots and things like that. Jake seemed pretty excited about it.

"He also spent hours after he went on the scouting missions with Captain Lewis documenting all the different new plants they found that nobody had ever seen before. They collected a bunch of samples. He spent lots of time drying and protecting those samples."

"Did he record where he found any of the samples?"

"Oh yeah, he drew little maps of the different stretches of the river and streams that flowed into the rivers and where the particular special plants grew. He put it all in the journal they kept in safe waterproof sacks. Captain Lewis and Lieutenant Clark drew bigger, more detailed maps on tanned animal hides that they rolled up and stored in the sacks.

"It was fun watching them come up with names for rivers and streams that nobody had ever named before, except maybe the Indians. They also named the plants and even some animals that no white people had ever seen."

"They must have had a good amount of journals with them," Grampa said.

"They took all they could carry, I guess."

"Tell me, Max, as far as you know, did they keep all the completed journals with them through the entire trip, or did they hide any away to be retrieved at a later date?"

"I personally didn't see them stash any away, but I heard Captain Lewis and Lieutenant Clark talk about having to cache a bunch of material and supplies before they started the trek over the Rocky Mountains. That's when they would have to give up the boats in exchange for horses. They were making plans to buy horses from the Indians at that time. Then they'd pick up all that stuff on their way back home."

"Did they say where they would build the cache?"

"No, but it would have to be between Fort Mandan and the eastern base of the Rockies along the Missouri River. There was much more to the trip than just the part that I got to see."

"You know, Max, that was just the beginning of a lifetime journey for our friend, Jake McAllister, or as he would later be called, Doctor Jacob Andrew McAllister. That journey put him on the pathway to change the way people think about medicine. Years later, his research helped modernize medical practices and procedures, and was accepted worldwide.

"But, I'm afraid some of his most important work, is lost. We must find it. And Max—that's where you come in. I want you to make another visit with Jake McAllister."

Wow, maybe he's going to let me start helping him find the lost documents.

"But," there was a hesitation on the line, "there's something very important we need to do first." There was a change in the tone of his voice—a much more serious tone.

"What's that?" I asked.

"There should be no more secrets in the family."

Uh-oh, this is gonna get complicated.

CHAPTER 11

"I'd been wondering when we'd get around to that," I said. "You know, I felt kinda guilty taking off on my adventures without my family knowing. It's kinda like I was doing stuff behind their backs. I really don't like doing that."

I felt a relief like a weight had been taken off my shoulders. I knew the family should be aware of what I was doing, but I didn't know how to bring it up with my grandfather.

"I'm glad you feel that way, Max. It's been my intention ever since you and I met to include the whole family in this. It must be done. I just needed to find the right time. The time is now, before you get more deeply involved in our work. I'll call your mom tomorrow night and invite the family over for dinner this weekend. It should be an interesting evening."

"So, what about my assignment with Doctor McAllister?" I asked.

There was a slight hesitation on the line. Then he said, "I want you to put that on hold until after we bring the family into this. That will be our next order of business."

The next night, as promised, Grampa called Mom. We were finishing up in the kitchen after dinner when the phone rang.

"That was your grandfather," Mom said as she put the kitchen phone back in its cradle. "He called to invite us over for dinner next Saturday. Says he has big, fat steaks on the menu."

"Oh boy! Grilling's my specialty, I said. Maybe Jeffery will let me grill."

"I'll bet that can be arranged," Mom said.

"Ya think Grampa will teach us some more magic," Megan grinned.

"Y'all shouldn't pester him about that," Dad said. "He'll get around to that when he wants to."

"Mom had a look on her face like she was trying to figure something out. "You know, he asked the strangest question before he got off the phone.

"What's that?" Dad asked.

"He wanted to know what women in history Megan and I admired."

Dad's eyebrows raised. "He just asked that out of the blue?" What did you tell him?"

"Well, I told him I'd always admired Helen Keller for everything she overcame, and I know Megan chose Clara Barton to do a report about in the ninth grade. When I asked him why he wanted to know, he just said he wanted to prepare a surprise for us."

"Boy, that old guy's full of surprises, isn't he?" Dad quipped.

I rolled my eyes. *You don't know the half of it.*

The next evening just after dinner, the phone rang again. I answered it.

"Hello?"

It was Grampa. "Hello, Max. Ask your mom or dad if it's okay if I stop by for just a second. I want to drop something off for your mom and Megan."

"Okay. Hey Dad," he was sitting next to me watching TV, "is it all right if Grampa comes by for a minute. He wants to drop something off."

"Of course, it is. He's welcome anytime."

"Good, I heard him," he said. "I'll be by in about 20 minutes."

Megan answered the doorbell and gave Grampa a hug as he came in. Mom was next in line for a hug. Dad and I stood to greet him and shake hands.

"I'm sorry to barge in on your evening like this, but I wanted to get something to the girls before the weekend," Grampa said. He held two books in his hand. They were both wrapped with a red ribbon. He handed them to Mom and Megan.

"What a nice surprise," Mom said, admiring the cover of a book about the life of Helen Keller.

"Wow," Megan said checking the cover of her book. "*The Life and Times of Clara Barton*. How cool! Thank you."

"Those were two very important ladies of their time," Grampa said. "The reason I brought them over tonight is because I'd like for you to start reading them before we get together this weekend. I think we'll have some interesting things to discuss. In each, you'll find a leather bookmark. Some people set their bookmark aside as they read. However, with these, it's very important that you keep the bookmark between the pages you're reading. You'll find the bookmark to be beneficial. If you'll indulge me that, and start reading your book tonight when you go to bed, I think you'll enjoy the experience."

He nodded, smiled, clasped his hands together and brought his forefingers to his lips. "So, with that, I'll leave you to enjoy the rest of your evening."

"Oh, Papa, won't you stay awhile," Mom said, reaching for his arm. "I can put on some coffee or there's brandy."

"No, no. I've imposed on your evening enough with no notice," he said patting her hand. "We'll have a nice visit Saturday."

"Thank you so much," Mom said reaching to him for another hug.

"I'll start mine tonight for sure," Megan said. "Thanks, Grampa."

Mom stood with her back to the door for a moment after Grampa left, looking at her book. She pulled the ribbon loose and opened the book, revealing the soft, leather bookmark.

"How interesting," she said. Look at the markings on this bookmark." She showed it to me and Dad. "Looks like some strange symbols have been imprinted or burnt into the leather. Wonder what they mean."

I kept my mouth shut as Mom, Dad and Megan examined the bookmarks. It was clear to me what was happening. It appeared that soon I would not be the only family member that shared Grampa's power.

I purposely didn't pick up the big book from my bedside table that night. I was tempted to, because of all the untapped adventures there, but that was not my night for adventure. Adventure that night belonged to Mom and Megan.

The almost full moon and cloudless sky left night shadows dancing on my bedroom walls as leaves on the tree outside were tossed by the gentle wind. The stillness of the night was broken only by the distant barking of a bored dog a block away responding to an imaginary threat.

It was deep in the early morning, and my mind was too busy to allow sleep. My bed sheet was a wad as I had tossed and turned, wondering how Mom and Megan were dealing with their first nocturnal time travel adventure. If it was anything like my first visit into the past, they will enjoy an adventure they remember only as a vivid dream.

I expected that Grampa was having a similar night as I; wondering and worrying about their first encounter with something as seemingly impossible as time travel. But I knew he accepted the fact that once he allowed me to peek inside his box of secrets, he would have to open it all the way and let the rest of the family in. I knew that whatever the results and their reaction would be, we would all be affected forever by it.

Finally, I managed to drift off to sleep and awoke a few hours later to the normal morning sounds of the house.

I found Mom in the kitchen, setting out fix-it-yourself breakfast food as usual. Dad, also as usual, had already left for work. Mom hummed a familiar tune while filling the coffee pot with water when I entered the kitchen.

"Morning, Max, she said tossing me a couple of oranges. "Would you cut up a few slices for us."

I reached for a knife in the drawer and got out the cutting board. "How was your night?" I asked casually as I started slicing.

"Good! She said looking up and smiling at me. Got a really good night's sleep for a change. I had the most interesting dreams though."

"Oh yeah? What about?"

"It's kinda strange. You know, I started reading that book that Papa dropped off about Helen Keller. Oh, what an inspirational woman she was. She overcame so much. Then I had the most detailed dream about her early life and the obstacles she overcame. It's so weird. I remember everything in the dream so vividly."

"Don't you dream on a regular basis?" I asked.

"Yes, but not like I did last night. Usually, I forget most of a dream by the time I wake up."

"What about dreams?" Megan said, brushing her hair, as he walked into the kitchen.

"Honey, don't brush your hair in the kitchen," Mom scolded.

"Oh, sorry," Megan shoved her brush into her PJ pocket. "Y'all were talking about dreams, What about them?"

"Mom was just telling me about her dream last night," I said.

"What about it?" Megan asked, reaching for the package of wheat bread to load the toaster.

Mom answered, "Like I was telling Max, I had this dream about what I read from the Helen Keller book Papa gave me."

"Shut. Up!" Megan said. She stood, bread in hand with a slack jaw looking at Mom. That's exactly what happened to me! I went to bed and read some from my new book. Then I dreamed about Clara Barton in the Civil War, taking care of wounded soldiers. It was so real. Just like I was there. For some reason though, I felt safe. I didn't feel scared at all. I've never had a dream that seemed so real."

"How did you feel when you woke up?" I asked.

"Normal—rested, but thinking about that dream. I can still tell you every detail that happened. I'm so sad for those soldiers, but that realistic dream was so cool. I'm telling you, I'm gonna have to do more reading."

"Max," Mom turned to me, "You've been reading some books that your Grampa gave you. Do you have dreams about them?"

"Yeah, sometimes," *Which is true.* "He's a really good writer." *That's also true.*

Mom stood holding a dinner knife loaded with peanut butter while she waited for the toast to pop up in the toaster. "It just seems a strange coincidence that Megan and I had the very same experience after reading the first few pages."

"Maybe you should ask him about it at his dinner," I said.

"I'll do that, she said. He's pretty smart. I'll bet he'll have an answer."

"Whatever the case," Megan said. "I'm reading more tonight. That's a really good book. Maybe I'll have another dream like last night."

My nerves were on edge during breakfast. I'll be so glad when this is all over. I felt bad that I was privileged to information that

Mom, Dad, and Megan were not. How will Grampa explain his secrets? How will they react? Will they be angry with him? Will they be angry with me? Probably both of us. I hope this doesn't fall apart. How will Dad react? I can expect that Megan will be furious with me because I got to do some really cool stuff and she didn't. Maybe I'm making too big a deal out of it. No, it *is* a big deal. I should be concerned—very concerned. But the whole thing is out of my hands now. I'll somehow just have to wait and see how it all unfolds at Grampa's dinner.

The next morning, I needed to get out of the house and try to clear my mind of the stress I had allowed to build up inside.

"Mom," I called as I headed out the door after breakfast, "I'm going to hang out with the guys, okay?"

"Fine Dear, have fun."

I grabbed my skateboard, gloves, helmet, knee and elbow pads, and Bungie strapped it all together to my bike and headed over to Jeremy's. He was still having breakfast, so I waited for him while he finished up his Cheerios and juice. Then we rode over to Rick's house.

"You sure you really want to do this?" Jeremy asked as we pedaled along the street.

I was silent a moment before I answered. "Yeah, I do. You know Rick is proud of what he and his dad made and he's offered to share it with us several times. Our friendship says we really need to do this."

"Yeah," Jeremy said, but I'm not into tempting death."

"Oh, now you're being overly dramatic. We haven't even seen the new build yet. And besides, Rick hasn't broken any bones so far this year."

Jeremy cut his eyes to me "So, maybe you'll be the first."

I rolled my eyes and kept riding.

Rick had been after us for weeks to try out the new Home Skate Park Extravaganza in his backyard he and his dad had expanded from the skate ramp they built last year. Jeremy and I had been putting him off because, quite honestly, Rick isn't the most safety conscious guy. Jeremy and I normally don't reach Rick's level of risk-taking. But that day, I needed something to focus on, rather than what was going to happen when Grampa opens his great big box of secrets to the family.

When we rolled into Rick's yard, we heard wheels against plywood and fiberglass in the backyard. We pushed open the side fence gate and there was Rick, oblivious to anything going on outside his immediate world. His earbuds were shoved in. His music was loud, some escaping beyond his ears. Half the backyard was occupied with elevated plywood and fiberglass ramps, a sixteen-foot-wide bowl, stairs and metal rails. It took us watching him a little while before he saw we had entered the yard.

Waving and grinning, he yelled, "hey guys, check this out." He made a sweeping loop around the edge of the bowl, arced up and over the top of a ramp and skittered down a metal rail next to a set of stairs, up off another ramp, and flew from the top edge of it onto their trampoline at the edge of the contraption. He caught his skateboard mid-air before his first bounce on the trampoline.

"Dang," I said, "you've really gotten good at this."

"I usually wipe out flying off the rail, he grinned."

"You made it that time," Jeremy said in admiration. "Looks like you've done it a million times. And what a fancy set up you have."

"Thanks," Rick chuckled. "Dad said he had trouble finding a stopping place while he was building it. Come on, guys, gear up. You've got some catching up to do."

We spent a couple of hours going through maneuvers under Rick's instruction. It was apparent that Rick was taking his skateboarding seriously. He'd obviously spent hundreds of hours practicing his moves over and over until he could do most of them without serious mishap. But we all fell multiple times. That's just part of it. Thankfully our safety gear kept us from getting anything more serious than a few minor bruises.

By noon we'd worked up a good sweat and hunger and headed down to Micky D's for burgers, fries and plenty of cold drinks. If we'd brought our swimsuits, we'd have gone to the city park pool for a dip, but instead, we rode on down to the river, shed our shirts and shoes and played around in the cool water in our shorts. Someone had tied a rope to a big tree limb that hung over the water. We did more than our share of swinging out over the water and splashing in off the rope. We pushed our luck several times challenging each other for different airborne stunts as we left the rope. We were thankful there were no careless incidents.

Thanks to the guys, I'd accomplished my goal of taking my mind off of matters having to do with the family and The House of Discovery. I was really tired by the time I got home from all the physical activity during the day.

I helped Mom with dinner, crashed by the TV with Dad after dinner to watch a baseball game, and went to bed during the seventh inning.

The next day went well and I kept busy working in the yard with Dad that morning and then going shopping with Mom for school clothes that afternoon. Mom had taken Megan shopping earlier in the week because Megan's part-time job at the florist kept her Saturdays occupied during business hours.

CHAPTER 12

Saturday evening arrived, and we were on Grampa's front porch, ringing his doorbell.

"Glad to see you. Come on in." Grampa welcomed us with a wide smile and open arms. After greetings and hugs, he led us to the kitchen/dining area of the great room. Jeffery came out from behind the kitchen island to greet us like we were all family. "What can I make for you to drink?" he asked.

"Why don't you surprise us," Dad said. "You're so creative with your wizardry around the kitchen and bar.

"Well, I'll just see what I can whip up then." He grinned and winked. Come on guys, give me a hand." Megan and I joined him at the bar, washed our hands and awaited his instruction. We helped him gather ingredients and set up the blender.

While we worked with Jeffery, Mom and Dad sat at the bar with Grampa, chatting about summer family activity and plans for the fall.

"In fact," Mom said, "we were just shopping for the kid's school clothes this week. Looks like summer will be over before we know it. Will you be going back to substitute teaching for the new semester?"

"No," Grampa said. "I stay busy enough right here." He ducked his head slightly and looked over the rims of his glasses. "You know I'm a little embarrassed to say this, but I had an ulterior motive for taking that job at the school library last spring for a few weeks."

"Oh, really? Mom said. "What's that?"

"Well, when I first learned that I had a family and you were here and that I indeed had grandchildren, I wanted more than anything to know you all. I wanted to be involved with you. I wanted to be close to you. So, I moved here to your little town. But I still couldn't come forward to meet you. After all those years I was afraid that I would scare you away. So, I decided that if I could just meet my grandchildren, maybe I could find a way to present myself to the rest of you. That's why I took the temporary job at the school. I hoped that if I put myself where my grandson was, perhaps I could meet him and through him, I could meet you all."

"So, you did, and we did, and we all lived happily ever after," Mom smiled, reached for Grampa and folded her arms around him for a long hug.

"Yes, happily ever after," Grampa said as Mom released her embrace. He lifted his hand and brushed it across his eye. "Hey," he said changing the subject. "How are those drinks coming along?"

"All done," I said. I reached across the bar and put napkins in front of Mom, Dad, and Grampa. Megan sat frosty drinks with a slice of pineapple resting on the rim on the napkins. Then Megan, Jeffery and I raised our cherry limeades.

"To family!" I said.

"To family," Dad repeated as they raised their glasses and we all drank to our family unity and happiness.

So, Grampa cracked his box of secrets open just a little by telling a secret about meeting me that even I didn't know. I thought about it a moment and realized I was okay with the way it all came down.

No, as a matter of fact, I was *more* than okay with it. I was really glad that he found me by whatever means, and through me, found the rest of the family.

"So, tell me, Papa," Mom said, "What are you working on in your studio these days? Making more jewelry?"

"No, not jewelry, but I do have something I've been working on that I'd like to show you. You've not seen my studio yet. Come on, let me give you a tour."

Grampa led us outside and along the paths lined with striking color in the gardens to his studio at the back of his property. Mom expressed that she thought that each new group of flowers were prettier than the ones we'd just passed.

Once inside the studio. Mom gushed with awe.

"Oh my gosh!' she said as she put her hand to her mouth. "Would you look at this." Her eyes darted from the well-lit, window-lined walls of the painting and sculpting areas to the back of the room where glass blowing and welding was done. Then she glanced to the other side of the large room at the state-of-the-art equipment in the wood shop and back to the tidy jeweler benches by the door.

"Papa, you've got everything a person could ever want for hobbies right here," Mom said, looking around, trying to take it all in at once.

Grampa grinned. "I'll have to say I do get a lot of enjoyment out here playing around. You know, you're all welcome to use any of this anytime you want."

"Oh, I could put in some serious time in that woodshop," Dad said, checking out the lathe and other table-mounted equipment.

"Look, Mom," Megan called, pointing to the sculpting area, "here's a potter's wheel. We could make cool pots and stuff."

I joined in. "I can see myself learning how to blow glass someday. I've seen people do it on TV. It looks really fun."

Grampa chuckled at everyone's enthusiasm for potential shop projects. "I hope you'll use it. There's some equipment that I just haven't had time to get around to using. It all needs regular use.

"I don't have much time for my hobbies, but it seems like I spend most of my time when I *am* out here in the painting and sculpting area. I like the way the light comes through the windows in the morning, giving me the natural light I need."

He walked across the floor and stood by an easel that had a white cloth draped over a canvas about two and a half feet square. It was set up next to a table loaded with brushes and paints. A stool sat next to it, ready to be used.

"This is my most recent project," he said as he reached for the cloth and removed it from the canvas.

I was standing at Grampa's side when he removed the cover. "Wow! Would you look at that," I said. My mouth hung open as I took it in.

The family gathered around to see what Grampa had unveiled.

"No way!" was all Megan could say.

"Oh my," Dad said, quietly shaking his head as he stared at the piece.

Mom was speechless as her hand again went to her mouth. She grabbed Grampa's arm and just held on as she admired his work.

The artwork that held us spellbound was a portrait done in acrylics of Megan and me that he did from a photo taken while we were camping. The color and light on our larger-than-life faces were blended in such a way that he made us look like we were about to break away from the canvas and burst out laughing. The painting was so life-like that our glistening eyes looked as if they would blink at any time. It was, by far, the best likeness of us I'd ever seen.

"That's just beautiful," Mom said.

"I hoped you'd like it, because it's yours." Grampa planted a kiss on Mom's forehead.

Later, after Mom calmed a bit from her euphoria about the painting, we returned to the house. Mom took charge of carefully carrying the painting.

Megan and I resumed our roles as assistant chefs to Jeffery to prepare a wonderful dinner of ribeye steaks and asparagus from the grill, twice baked potatoes from the oven, and a crisp garden salad. Jeffery also prepared a real surprise for the end of the meal. Along with rich Kona coffee, he served a wonderful chocolate and caramel turtle pie, garnished with walnuts and shaved chocolate on top. The dinner was as enjoyable to eat as it was to prepare.

Good steaks are easy to over or under-cook, but I was proud of the compliments I got for what Grampa called my *mastery of the grill.*

Jeffery had the table cleared and things put away in the kitchen by the time we finished our desserts. He excused himself when Grampa invited us to relax in the large family room. We gathered in a comfortable conversation area around the fireplace.

Grandpa poured apricot brandy for Mom and Dad and asked Dad if Megan and I could have a little. Dad responded by showing about a quarter of an inch between his finger and thumb.

After pouring drinks into the small glasses, Grampa settled into his chair and looked around to see that everyone was relaxed in the soft leather upholstery.

His eyes fell on Mom. The corners of his lips raised slightly in that knowing smile I'd seen before. "Tell me, Susan, did you and Megan have an opportunity to read any from the books that I dropped off for you?"

"Yes," Mom said without hesitation. "We talked about it the next morning. We agreed that we really liked the stories, though they were both sad, what we read anyway."

Megan nodded her agreement.

Mom continued, "And we'll be finishing them for sure, but we shared some unexpected and extraordinary experiences afterward."

Grampa ran his fingers through his beard. "Tell me more."

"We both had the coolest dreams about what we read," Megan blurted out. "They were so vivid—so real. We remembered every detail."

Mom added, "Yes, but the strangest thing is that we both had the same experience—such strong memories of our dreams."

"Did you enjoy the experience?" Grampa asked.

"Boy, I'll say!" Megan exclaimed. "It was like being right in the middle of a 3-d movie."

"She's right," Mom agreed.

Grampa's well-groomed beard spread across his face with his best smile.

"That—is what I want to talk about tonight."

CHAPTER 13

Grampa's eyes were clear with that little twinkle he gets when he's especially enthusiastic about something. He sat in his wing-backed chair, leaning slightly forward with both feet on the floor. He restrained animation with his hands by keeping them folded in his lap.

"What I'm about to tell you is absolutely true. What you will hear may sound so outrageous and incredible, you'll have trouble believing it. But believe me, it's all true. I will show you what would appear to be impossible is possible.

"As you already know, I'm a magician. I—we—" he made a circular gesture with his hand that included me, Megan and Mom, "share certain powers that come with our ancestry. I've worked all my life to develop those supernatural powers to give me the ability to do things that few people have even attempted, much less achieved. We talked about some of those powers on the camping trip and I demonstrated a little example of levitation and transport.

"For years I experimented with those powers in many different ways. Finally, after thousands of hours of research and experimentation, I learned how to combine and channel very specific supernatural powers with some highly advanced scientific factors to take even farther what most people would consider inconceivable."

He adjusted his position slightly in his chair, filled his lungs and exhaled slowly before continuing.

"I've broken the barrier of time travel." He hesitated a moment and looked each of us in the eyes to allow what he just said soak in. "No, I cannot travel into the future. The future is and always will be a mystery to everyone. But just the opposite is true with the past.

"Our history speaks to us through its fossils, architecture, forgotten ruins, artifacts, religion, legends and the written word. Entire civilizations have risen and fallen in the past. Some have been documented, many not. Scientists and researchers have been limited in what they could learn about the past to only what they could uncover through historical and archeological research—digging up old bones and artifacts and spending years analyzing them.

"However, I've developed a method to very safely—let me repeat—*very safely* visit a specific time, location, event and individual person in the past. I can observe first-hand from the viewpoint of that person, exactly what happened in their time and place. Then, when the visit is complete and the information that was sought has been obtained, I can return, *again very safely,* home with all the information gleaned from the mission intact.

"Now, what does that have to do with you and the books I gave you and your dreams?"

Mom's body language and facial expression said, *I believe him, but this sounds absolutely crazy.*

Megan's jaw was slack but taking on an expression that said, *is this for real?*

125

Dad was harder to read. *Very skeptical but leaving an opening in his mind for more information.*

Me? How was I reacting? I already knew everything he was saying was absolutely true, but I restrained from nodding agreement to his comments.

Grampa continued, "Those *'dreams'* (he used air quotes) you experienced weren't dreams at all." Again, he hesitated. "You were indeed remembering the time travel experience you had."

"What?!" Mom almost came out of her chair.

I've only seen Mom come really unglued just a couple of times in my life.

"What do you mean, we had a time travel experience? Papa, you're scaring me. Are you saying that you sent my daughter and me off on some wild time travel trip?"

"Susan," Grampa said in a soothing voice, "just calm down, listen, and I'll explain.

"I believe that I'm obligated to share the knowledge and power I have with you and the children. I can't share it with anyone else—only those with my genes. It will all die with me if I can't share it with you. I can't go to my grave and take this wonderful secret with me. I at least want you to understand the gift that I have for you, Megan and Max and how to use it.

"If I were to try to explain what my time travel capability is all about without you actually experiencing it first-hand yourself, you absolutely wouldn't believe me—*but* you can't deny the experience you had. It was real. You actually went back in time. You became a part of Helen Keller as a child and young woman. You experienced the pain and frustration inside her because you were her for a

period of time. You actually lived it. You were there. Then you came back home safely. It all happened exactly the way you remember it. You caused no harm to your host and no harm could possibly come to you. Your host had no knowledge of your visit. In no way can you control her behavior, and you absolutely in no way can affect any change in history.

"So, as clumsy and awkward as I have made this explanation, what I'm offering is a very special gift, and I hope you and Tom will let Megan and Max experience it and learn how to take advantage of all it has to offer."

Megan got up from the couch beside me and went to the other sofa to squeeze in between Mom and Dad. She took Mom's hand and held it between hers.

"Mama, I read from my book again last night and had the same reaction we both had the night before. I remember very distinctly how it felt to be Clara Barton in that battlefield hospital, no more than a shack really, with cannons blasting all around while she tried to help wounded and dying men. Mama, I saw, tasted, heard and felt all of it. I heard the cannon blasts, the bullets flying around, and the men crying for water and help to ease their pain. I saw the terrible things that happen in war and tried as much as I could to give comfort to those hurting so badly from their injuries. That was no dream. After what Grampa just told us, I know I was there. I was Clara Barton for a while. Mama, that was one terrible experience for me, but I wouldn't take anything for it. I want more. Not more war, of course, but I want to have the ability to see the good things that happened in the past too. I think

Grampa can give that to us. Please, Mama, Daddy, let him do that. I believe in him."

I was keeping my mouth shut. It looked like Mom was calming down and heard what Megan had to say. I didn't think it would be a good time to tell her that I'd been taking time travel trips with Grampa for a couple of months without her knowledge. Maybe we could squeeze that into a conversation later, down the road. Dad was still being hard to read. Hopefully, he was leaving the door open.

The room was silent for a moment while they thought about what Megan said. Then Grampa smiled and broke the silence.

Looking at Mom and Dad, he said, "Susan and Tom, you should be so proud of your children, and I certainly understand you being protective of them. They're two of the finest young people I've ever known. And I'm not saying that because they're my grandkids. They will grow to become fine adults, regardless of any involvement with me. But there's a power and an untapped source of inherited energy within them that if understood and developed could give them unlimited opportunity to be the very best at whatever they pursue in life. There could be no boundaries to their success. Susan, you have the same genes as the children. You, also, can learn to be the best you can be."

"I just want to be a good mom and wife," Mom said, looking around at us.

"I'd say you're already that, Grampa said, "but you can be much more if you want.

"You know," he continued, "just introducing Max and Megan to the powers within them will stimulate their curiosity. That, in turn, starts the processes to increase their intellect, creating a cycle of life-long learning.

"We can turn that key that will open a whole new world of exploration for them—intellectual exploration and thrilling experiences through time travel."

After listening quietly to everything Grampa said, Dad finally broke his silence in his, *let's get to the chase,* way.

"Alright, let's just assume for a moment that you're not a total nut case, and let's just assume—just assume, mind you, that you have indeed found a way to time travel. So, what's in all this for you? You wouldn't be doing all this unless you had a darn good reason."

"You're absolutely correct, Grampa nodded. "I do have a very good reason. As you know, I've spent my career primarily as a historian and archeologist, researching, seeking artifacts, and writing about historical events. I've also studied the physical sciences in great depth.

"Years ago, I learned that some very accomplished people in the past, including some of my ancestors; people who made significant scientific discoveries for their time, hid away documentation of some of their most important breakthroughs before they died. Some of their discoveries were many decades, even centuries ahead of their time. They hid those documents because the world, and science at the time, was not ready for their advanced discoveries. Many are still too advanced to be unveiled. They knew if their discoveries were found by forces of evil or greed, and used improperly the world could be doomed.

"You see, I have made it my life work to find and protect those books of discovery from the forces of evil. That's what we do. My staff and I find and protect these treasures of the past until scientific research of the future catches up with those discoveries and can use them for the betterment of mankind."

"Staff? What staff?" Dad said, looking around the room with both hands raised in the air, like, *where's the staff?*

Grampa smiled, "This house isn't exactly as it appears. You'll meet the staff later."

"Looks to me like very little around here is as it appears, including you," Dad said in a tone I'd never heard before.

"Please bear with me, Tom," Grampa continued, "I know this is unsettling to you. I'll explain everything. There's much more you need to understand.

"Yes, I have a small staff. They do the preliminary research, but only I, because of my supernatural ability can travel back in time to seek the details necessary to find the lost books.

"So, why involve our family? Simply put—I need help. Susan, Megan, and Max have the built-in capability to time travel like I do, and perhaps help with the research.

"You see, we've been successful in finding and protecting a good number of lost books, documents, and a storehouse of very special artifacts. But there are many more leads we're turning up. With me as the only one able to travel in time to verify those leads, we're leaving an untold number of lost documents unprotected.

"Now to add a sense of urgency to everything I've told you, we've recently learned that a distant relative, a man with somewhat similar powers as mine, but a very evil person, is looking for the same lost documents." Grampa's face took on a grim look. "I don't intend to be overly dramatic here, but I've researched this man. I know what he's capable of doing. If he gets to them before we do, it could spell doom for the world as we know it."

My heart stood still while I waited for Dad to respond.

Dad's face drained of color. "So, you're saying my kids, by helping you find these lost documents could—*save the world?*"

Grampa looked Dad squarely in the eyes, "Tom, that's exactly what I'm saying."

I looked across at Megan, sitting between Mom and Dad. Her eyes were as big as mine. *Did he say, "save the world?*

CHAPTER 14

Grampa waited a moment for that last bombshell to filter through our brains.

Then he stood and took a few steps to stand at the corner of the couch beside me. He looked down at me and took a deep breath.

"There's one more piece of information that I need to share with you in order to provide total transparency about this whole matter. It involves Max."

Oh boy, here it comes. It's gonna hit the fan now.

"As you know," Grampa continued, "Max and I met at the school library. He needed a book for a class project having to do with Texas history. I knew him immediately as my grandson but didn't want to, as he would say, *freak him out*, by revealing it to him at that time. He didn't learn that until I shared it with all of you at the same time. I did, however, want him to get the best information available, delivered in the best way possible way about the material for his history report. So, I gave him a special book with a very special bookmark—like those I gave to you. I knew it would be perfectly harmless to him and the benefits could be immeasurable."

Mom interrupted with an edge of anger in her voice, "It's not your place to determine what may be harmless or beneficial to our son. That's for his dad and me to decide."

I knew her Mama Bear side would come out over this.

"Susan, take it easy for a moment," Grampa said. "Please let me finish. I expected that you and Tom might be upset over something that you wouldn't understand. That's why I asked that Max allow me to share this information with you. That's what we're doing tonight."

Mom sighed, and her face softened slightly as she sat back to hear Grampa out.

He continued. "Max's reaction to reading the chapters about Texas history was much the same as yours. At first, it just seemed like very vivid dreams of what he read. Then, he realized it was much more than that. When he confronted me about it, I shared everything with him that I've told you tonight, except the part about him and his sister having the capability to save the world.

"What I haven't told him yet is something I wanted to share with all of you. His exposure and awareness to the powers within him has already started giving him an edge, a special boost so to speak that enhances his ability to focus. It improves his memory and makes learning easier. He's a smart kid already. This won't make him an overnight genius, but in time, who knows. It can help open doors and give him the confidence to succeed at whatever he pursues. And, the more he understands and develops those powers, the greater his intellect will develop.

"The same holds true with Megan. I know she's a good student now. Good study habits and good grades are a part of who she is, but perhaps she may want to spread her wings, to look at new avenues to investigate. Quite honestly, the sky's the limit for these two."

Mom looked thoughtfully at me and then Grampa. Her ire was quick to rise and just as quick to cool.

"You know," she said, "Max's grades had always been B's and C's, but his last report card was mostly A'a and only a couple of B's—no C's at all. We were very proud of him. Was that because of all this?"

"Yes, I would say so," Grampa said. "Max, what do you think?"

I thought a moment and looked at Mom. "Like I told you when the report cards came out, I do seem more focused. Things seem a little easier for me. I just enjoyed school more since I started reading Grampa's books."

Grampa tilted his head to the side, looked over the tops of his glasses, lifted his hands palms up, chest high, and made a gesture that said, *So, there you are.*

I could tell that Grampa felt relieved the pressure was off. The big box of secrets was fully opened and the contents spread among my family. I felt very good about that.

Now, in a noticeably different and almost carefree mood, Grampa said, "Since you know what we do and why we do it, please let me show you where we do it."

He led us beyond the large living area, past the dining room, beside the expansive kitchen and the large study to the wide hallway at the rear of the house. The walls on either side were white, built-in display cabinets. They were artfully arranged with beautiful sculptures and artifacts. Most looked really old.

"What I'm going to show you," he said, "only a handful of other people have seen. You must understand the nature of what we do requires the utmost in secrecy and security. Those that work with me are small in number, but they are the best in the world at what they do. They've met and exceeded all the requirements of the most rigorous background investigation known to man. I trust them explicitly.

"You're seeing this because you are of my blood. Within you is all the power that I have developed in myself. It's just a matter of you learning how to draw it out and use what you already have. With all of today's technology and new scientific developments that can be combined with your untapped magic, I expect that you'll far exceed what I've done with the ability you can develop."

Megan and I looked at each other with grins that said, *can you believe this?*

"So, come with me," Grampa said, "and I'll show you the heartbeat of the House of Discovery." He reached for a piece of sculpture on one of the display shelves. He rested his hand on the top of a stately looking bronze horse head. The art piece looked like it could have been cast a thousand or more years ago, perhaps in the Mid-East or Asia. He tweaked one of the horse's ears and the entire shelving cabinet started silently sliding into the wall. Behind the secret door was an alcove with what looked like elevator doors in the middle of the wall in front of us.

Megan couldn't help herself as she squeaked, "Oh my goodness," when she stepped into the elevator alcove.

Once inside the alcove, Grampa pushed the elevator button. Not only did the elevator doors open, but the secret door that was made to look like a cabinet slid closed.

I had no sense of how far we traveled in the elevator. The movement indicated that we were going down rather than up. After the initial surge, the car moved so smoothly and quietly, I couldn't tell if we moved twenty feet or eighty feet into the ground. When the door opened, we faced a brightly lit passageway about eight-feet-wide, eight-feet-high, and fifty-feet-long. The ceiling and both walls were finished with white, shiny tile. The floor was smooth, resin-coated concrete. There were three doors. One was at the end of the hallway and the other two were situated midway between the elevator and the door at the end. I saw no less than four security cameras mounted in strategic locations along the corridor. I knew we were being watched.

"I know it looks a little cold and unwelcoming here," Grampa said, "but it's all for security purposes. You'll get used to it."

If I could have seen myself at the time, I probably looked scared. I looked from one side of the pristine hallway to the other. I'm sure my mouth was hanging open as we passed the doors midway to the end of the hall.

All the way through the elevator ride and the walk along the gleaming white tile of the deep underground passageway, Megan was wide-eyed and slack-jawed. Mom and Dad were quiet but obviously impressed as Grampa led the tour. I was in awe of the place.

When we reached the door at the end of the corridor, Grampa placed his right palm with his fingers outstretched onto a glass security plate. It was mounted on the wall about shoulder-high and was shaped like a hand. He also looked into an iris reading instrument. It took only a second or two for the security devices to sync and buzz us through the door. He pushed it open and ushered us in.

I didn't know what I expected to find beyond the door, but what I did see was amazing. Mom's and Dad's eyes popped wide in astonishment. Megan emitted a long, drawn out, "Wow!" as she looked around.

The large room literally hummed from small cooling fans inside the array of electronic equipment cabinets. It was filled with open workstations loaded with computers, monitors and racks full of electronic boxes and gadgets. Tiny yellow and green lights faintly flickered on the front panels as the equipment did whatever it did. The handful of computer workstations were in a semi-circular area where the operators could converse and share work information. One wall was covered with monitors obviously connected to security cameras. There must have been twenty or so cameras scanning the property both inside and out from every possible angle. Other screens were filled with historical documents, records, and maps.

I recognized two of the four operators at their workstations. One was Jeffery, Grampa's houseman and cook. The other was Hatch, the military looking guy I thought was the gardener and part-time researcher. There were two others I didn't know working at their stations.

"Welcome to our operations center," Grampa said proudly. "This is where we do our research and try to unravel the past. Let me introduce you to the team." The people working stopped what they were doing when we entered the room. All wore warm, welcoming expressions.

"We are so fortunate to have these people as our team members," Grampa said. "Each of them brings their own set of awesome skills."

He nodded to Hatch. "Mike Hatcher, we call him Hatch, is a retired Marine top gunnery sergeant and weapons expert. He's seen more than his share of action fighting terrorism in the Middle East and Africa. He got most of his advanced education while in the military, but finished with his masters in history with a minor in research methods after he retired from the Marine Corps. His hobby is horticulture. He's the genius that created our gardens outside." Hatch shook everybody's hand and patted me on the back.

"Jeffery here is Doctor Jeffery Hollister, Ph.D. Of course, you already know Jeffery. If you thought he was just our great chief, he's much more than that. He earned his masters at Harvard with double majors in physics and chemistry. Then he changed direction slightly and earned his Ph.D. in ancient studies at Cambridge. He's been a tremendous asset helping us connect the dots we find in our research. He's also a world-class chef who enjoys tempting us with his special dishes, especially his desserts. As you know, he specializes in Island cuisine. He loves to treat us to full blown dinner parties from time to time." Jeffery shook our hands and hugged Mom and Megan.

"It's nice to know the boss's grandkids are such good cooks," Jeffery said. "I can sure use more help around here."

Grampa turned to the petite woman standing next to Jeffery. "Next, I want you to know Katherine Collins, a former intelligence officer with the U. S. Army. We call her Kat. Kat is a first-class researcher and IT specialist. She installed and keeps our equipment functional and finds innovative ways to enhance our research methods. She doesn't just ride a desk. She was very hands-on in three different Middle Eastern and African war zones installing key communication and IT equipment. Oh, and by the way, don't let her size fool you. She's an award-winning competitive martial artist." An attractive, smiling, dark-haired woman around thirty-five years old reached for our hands to shake. "So glad to know the boss's family," she said, smiling.

Grampa gestured to the large man standing beside Kat. "And finally, last, but certainly not least, this imposing gentleman is Rocky Taa." The six-foot-four, two hundred and seventy-pound Samoan thrust his muscled and tattooed arm and ham-like hand out to shake. As I shook hands with him, I noticed he stood on a prosthetic right leg under his cargo shorts.

Grampa continued. "Rocky's an ace researcher and our security specialist. He's also a former college star athlete and a Chief Petty Officer with the Navy SEALs. Unfortunately, he lost his leg below the knee in Afghanistan while saving his insertion team when a rescue mission went bad. By the way, they got all the good guys out. Rocky never sat around feeling sorry for himself. He can still keep up with most professional football rookie receivers in a fifty-yard dash using his prosthetic spring-type foot, and he continues to defend his championship for the all-Navy veteran arm wrestling contest every year in Washington, DC."

"Nice to meet you all," Rocky said.

"So," Grampa's eyes darted between his team members, "this is the team that helps me find and protect the books of discovery and other treasures. That's our goal. Usually, it's just routine research. Frequently though, we manage to dig up something that leads to a major discovery.

"When their research turns up something worthy of more investigation, I travel to that time and place to try to uncover the rest of the information we need to find what we're looking for. Then, if it pans out, we'll develop private archeological sites, if necessary, to dig into the past to uncover the treasures.

"Occasionally we hit the jackpot and find not only the documents we're looking for but long-lost and forgotten ancient treasures and works of art. That's the primary way we fund the operation."

We said our goodbyes to our new friends and Grampa ushered us back out the security door.

"Wow!" I said shaking my head in awe at what I'd just seen. "That's gotta be the coolest place in the entire world to work."

"I suspect you'll think the next couple of places I show you will be pretty *cool* too," Grampa chuckled.

CHAPTER 15

We stood in the passageway between the doors about halfway to the elevator. Grampa turned to the door on the right side. The security features on it looked like those that protected the operations center. He again gained entry using his palm, fingerprints and eye scanning. The door buzzed and automatically opened, allowing us entrance.

It was a large lounge and recreation area. To my right were comfortable couches, chairs, and tables clustered together for conversation and entertainment. A huge TV screen took up a large portion of that wall. I guessed they used it for watching movies and regular TV.

The other side of the room was filled with foosball, pool tables, and electronic game stations. It also included a complete gym with all types of work-out equipment from free weights to exercise machines. A hydration station and snack bar were along the wall. No furniture was situated between the door and the back wall at the far end of the room. Five round columns were evenly spaced along that wall. Between the columns were large wall panels. The panels were illuminated with subtle hidden lights and decorated with colorful abstract art reflecting athletes of different sports executing the moves they do best. No furniture, neither couches, chairs, or tables lined that wall—just the panels and columns.

Grampa stood by the door and leaned on a polished, wooden countertop as we wandered around the room, brushing our fingers along the expensive upholstered furniture, tables, and cabinets, taking it all in.

I thought about how cool it would be to be able to hang out and work in a place like this. I walked across the room to touch some of the exercise equipment. My eyes were wide with wonder.

"This is really neat," Megan said. "Just think of all the fun we could have here. Those people must really like working here."

"I'm very fortunate to have been able to attract such a fine group of professionals. I've tried to give them everything they need to get their jobs done and enjoy being here."

Mom asked, "Are the ones we met the only people that work for you?"

"No, I have a couple of trusted retired archeology professor friends that I manage to coax out of retirement occasionally to manage digs a few weeks at a time when necessary. Of course, they work at remote locations and never come here. I occasionally travel to their dig sites to work with them.

"There are also four other operations staff members who are currently on their rest rotation. You'll meet them later. You see, this is a seven day a week operation. Sometimes the job becomes very demanding. They work hard on a one-one rotation; one week on and one whole week off. They need the away time. It helps them recharge, so to speak. When they return to work, they're refreshed and ready for another work cycle. But it's not all work for them here. Although they are here, on site, 24/7 for their work, they have their rest and recreation hours. They all have hobbies that break up the intensity of the work. Their private quarters are upstairs.

"You already know that Jeffery enjoys cooking and managing social events, and Hatch manages the care of the gardens. Kat, like me, enjoys the creative arts. She sculpts and paints in the studio. And Rocky, when he's not working out with the gym equipment, does origami. That's the Japanese art of creatively folding papers into beautiful shapes and scenes. Rocky also designed and decorated this recreation center. Pretty impressive, huh? Any other questions?"

"Yes," Dad said. "It was impossible not to notice the strong military and security backgrounds of your team members, along with their scientific and research experience. Just what role does the military and security part play here?"

"That's a very good question, Tom, that I'll answer in a few minutes. First, though, I think what you'll see next will put your question in better perspective."

He ushered us back into the hallway and to the other security door across from the lounge. He again went through the eye and palm security process. When the door opened, it led into a roomy, steel reinforced, concrete-walled alcove that housed a massive stainless-steel bank-type vault door at the far end. I was impressed!

"This is the vault where the discoveries are housed," Grampa said. "With all the levels of security we have here, this is one of the safest places on earth to protect them. They'll stay here until such time that modern science will be able to understand and utilize knowledge they contain. The science defined in some of these documents is much too complex for the world's best technical and scientific minds of today. Someday though, the world will be a much better place because of that science, as long as we maintain this level of security."

An electronic keypad and a strange looking monitor with a slightly cup-shaped screen a little smaller than the size of a basketball were mounted to the wall inside the door. Grampa entered a long string of numbers and letters into the keypad. A gentle sounding woman's voice spoke to him from a hidden speaker somewhere around the monitor.

"Good evening," she said. "Please place the tip of your nose on the red indicator at the center of the screen."

Grampa stepped up to the monitor and gently pressed the tip of the nose against the bright red triangle that suddenly appeared at the center of the screen.

"Very good," The warm voice said. "Now please remain still with your eyes open while Identi-Scan verifies your identity."

A series of tiny red, green and yellow lights flickered all around Grampa's face for a few seconds. He looked a little funny— kinda like he stuck his head in a Christmas tree. I looked at Megan and grinned. Her expression said she must have had the same thought.

"Thank you, Doctor Magas. Please enter," the voice said.

We heard a loud, metallic click at the vault door.

Grampa walked the few steps to the massive wheel on the door. He grasped it and turned it to the left like he was steering a huge ship.

"The security system here is state of the art," he said. "The little lights you saw flashing were reading my bone structure, tissue depth, skin contours, and other details like skin color, moles, wrinkles, and so on."

He turned the big wheel as far as it would go until we heard another loud click. Then he gave a gentle tug on the immense vault door. It was balanced so perfectly, it swung outward as easily as a luxury car door.

Standing beside the open vault door, he gestured for us to enter.

"This is why we exist," he said leading us through the door.

Air escaped from my lips as words failed me with what we saw.

"This is fantastic," Megan gushed.

"Oh, my goodness," Mom stood in wonderment, looking around the room.

Dad must have been too awestruck to respond to what we saw.

Row upon row of gleaming stainless-steel tables with wide walkways between them covered the floor of the large concrete bunker. The walls were lined with floor to ceiling display cases enclosed with shaded glass fronts. The room temperature was cool—almost to the point of being uncomfortable. The lighting was dim; sort of like twilight. Resting on each table was a clear, plexiglass cube with several flexible tubes attached to the top surface and hinged doors on the fronts. The cubes were of various sizes. Some were as small as eighteen inches wide on each side.

Others were much larger; up to three feet per side. Scattered on the tables, between the cubes, were several computers, microscopes, and circular, lighted, magnifying instruments. There must have been close to a hundred of those cubes on the tables. About half of them toward the rear of the room appeared to be empty. The rest; those that met us when we entered the large room, were loaded with every type of writing material one could imagine.

Grampa stood silent for what seemed like a long time but really was just a moment while we took in the totality of the room.

"These," he said proudly, spreading his arms wide, "are our books of discovery and other treasures." He led us slowly among the tables describing the different types of documents housed in the protective cubes.

"As you can see, our books and documents come in every format imaginable. Some of our oldest are made of clay and stone tablets with figures etched into them. Others are made of very fragile papyrus sheets. Some papyrus comes in long scrolls while others are a series of single sheets. A few of the ancients recorded their discoveries on tanned animal leather. Along with stone and clay tablets, our best-preserved ancient documents are crafted from carefully processed sheepskins made into fine parchment. Such things as palm leaves and birch bark have also been used in the past for writing materials. We even have a couple of examples of ancient writings on thin copper scrolls.

He continued to explain the treasures as we walked slowly along the wide aisleways. "As time progressed, people eventually learned to make paper from linen threads, and then from other types of rags. The use of paper allowed sheets to be bound in leather covers for protection resembling books we know today. Many of those lasted centuries in their original environment.

"This collection is protected in this low light, temperature and humidity controlled dry atmosphere. Filtered nitrogen gas is added to their enclosures through those tubes you see to further reduce the moisture content and other contaminants.

"Modern paper is made from wood chips and other wood products and is much more user-friendly, as they say, than any of its predecessors. We've collected a few books made from paper similar to what we know today.

"It's taken a lifetime to research, physically locate, extract, translate, and electronically duplicate what you see here. Many of these volumes hold scientific secrets that can change the world for the better when the world's science is ready for it. That's why they're so precious and must be protected."

"Wow!" Dad said. "What a collection."

"This is unbelievable," Mom said. "But I believe it. You said you make electronic duplicates of all these. Where do you keep those?"

"Deep inside a granite mountain, far away in one of the most secure locations on earth. They're very safe." Grampa smiled with confidence.

"So, what's inside those big cases along the walls," Mom asked.

"Occasionally, when we go after these documents, we sometimes stumble onto other treasures. One can imagine that if a king or other royalty, or a wealthy merchant, or perhaps even a wizard or scientist was hiding valuables from a conquering army, or enemy, or for one of the many other reasons people hide things, they would include their most valuable treasures." He walked across the room and stood beside a row of cabinets along the wall that extended around the perimeter of the room.

He picked up a remote control from a table next to the display cases and pressed a button, illuminating the interior of the first cabinet. The inside light made the front glass transparent. "These are some of the riches we've uncovered along with those very special documents. He pressed the button again and held it down while each display case, in sequence, illuminated, exposing lighted glass shelves loaded with the most fabulous collection of art and riches from the ancient past that one could imagine." Mother's hand flew to her mouth as she gasped in astonishment. Dad, Megan and I gawked silently as we took in the room with amazement.

We followed Grampa as he walked slowly along the line of display cases. They were loaded with the most extraordinary sculptures, paintings, and artifacts of all types and sizes from all over the world. They were separated by the culture from which they came. There were vast amounts of jewelry and small figurines made of gold. Many pieces were studded with precious gems. Some beautiful sculptures were made of marble and granite. Other cast artwork pieces were of materials including copper and bronze. Rare European and Asian paintings from the middle ages and earlier times were on bold display. Scattered among the smaller artifacts were loose jewels laid out on velvet. Some were cut and polished, others appeared to be raw stones to be made into jewels.

Grampa watched our reactions for a moment and continued, "After we pay off the dig site property owners, local, regional, and national officials significant amounts in taxes, bribes, and kickbacks, there's still tremendous value in each piece. The potential value of this collection is unfathomable.

"This is the finest collection of ancient art in the world," he continued. The pieces in this collection have never been publicized, so the art community as a whole knows nothing of it. Once a year I make just a few pieces available to a small number of very discriminating wealthy collectors at a private sale. Thankfully, they clamor for an opportunity to bid on them. That's how we obtain our funding. We've quietly found, retrieved, tucked away and protected enough of these fascinating pieces over my career to assure that funds will be available for maintaining this facility and all the research and recovery that goes with it for as long as it's needed, well beyond our lifetimes—hopefully forever. Every year, new pieces continue to be added to the collection.

"So now you see the lost documents and everything they mean to us are not the only need for the secrecy and security. There's a massive fortune in artwork that we protect here as well.

"Yes Tom, to answer your earlier question, we've made sure each of the team members can not only dig deep for research results, but can exercise their well-honed ability *if necessary,* to defend and protect the treasures we've gathered here. We have ample means and equipment for them to do so, and they train regularly.

"So, any questions before we head back upstairs?"

"Yes, Mom said, "after showing us all of this, there's no way we cannot be impressed. You said you need help. Tell us, just what is it you want us to do?"

"In the beginning, I'd like for you to just do what you did the other night. Simply go to bed and read your book to take the little visits to the past like Max has done. It can only benefit you. It certainly can't hurt you. Get comfortable with the process of going back and forth in time. Learn, be entertained, enjoy yourself. Realize just how safe the process is. If you want to research someone else or visit some other event from the past, let me know and I'll get you the materials you'll need. You'll watch history actually happen from the eyes of a person living in the past, then wake up totally refreshed with complete recall of the entire adventure.

"Then, after you get some time travel and adventures under your belt, and allow everything we've talked about to digest, if you decide you want to continue, I'll give you specific assignments for additional journeys. I'll ask you to look into the lives of specific people with a list of factors and activities to look for. It will take no time or effort on your part because your physical self will be sound asleep while all that's going on.

"If you're curious about how all of this works, I'll explain the particulars of the technology as we progress and you learn more about your powers. I don't want to load you down with a lot of technical details all at once. I know this is a lot to take in."

He hesitated a moment and looked intently at Mom and Dad. "But, if after careful consideration, you decide that you don't want anything more to do with this, I'll be disappointed, but I've been disappointed before. I don't want you to feel coerced about any of it. You'll always be my family, whatever you decide. Fair enough?" He looked hopeful at all of us.

We were all silent for a moment until Mom spoke. "I guess that's about as fair as it can get," she said.

"With that, I'll escort you back upstairs," Grampa said, hugging Mom closely as they headed outside the vault door.

When we were upstairs, Mom retrieved her new portrait, and we all said our goodbyes with hugs.

Before closing the front door, Grampa said, "I just want you all to be totally comfortable with this. Talk about it and call me when you're ready."

CHAPTER 16

The silence in the car going home was deafening. I waited for someone to say something. They didn't.

Finally, I said, "Boy, that was something, wasn't it?"

"Max," Dad said, "I think we should hold our opinions on this whole thing while we all think about it. I believe it's best that your mom and I discuss this thoroughly. Then we'll all talk about it. Understand?"

"Yes, sir."

It's not often that Dad shuts me down like that. I didn't know if he was angry with me for getting involved with Grampa's time travel without letting them know or what. If he was, I understand. He had every right to be. He and I talk about everything. But I was in the middle of it before I knew I was actually taking the trips, just like Mom and Megan.

It was late, and Megan and I both went to our rooms as soon as we got home. I really wanted to talk to her about the whole situation with Grandpa. I wanted to know how she felt about it, but I wouldn't disobey Dad by talking to her about it. I felt sure we'd have a family meeting about it soon. I just didn't know when.

I heard muffled voices coming from Mom and Dad's room late into the night. I couldn't hear what they were saying, but at times, the muted voices sounded like they were arguing.

I couldn't in all conscience go to Grampa's big book to get away on an adventure in another time until our family crisis was solved. So, I tossed and turned for what seemed like hours wondering what direction Mom and Dad would take. Would they refuse to allow us to continue with Grampa's plan?

That man I now call Grampa came into our lives and totally changed what we thought our future would be.

Before we knew him, we were a regular family living our lives like most people. Megan and I were just kids growing up, not sure what our future held for us, and in reality, not really thinking much about it, at least me, anyway. Megan was a bit more goal-driven than me.

Grampa then gave us an opportunity out of the blue that could totally change who we are and what we could do. That whole concept and everything that went with it was not only mindboggling to me but frightening as well.

But what scared me more was if the forces of evil gained possession of those powerful secrets that Grampa protected. That scared the daylights out of me.

The decision our family needed to make was very clear to me. I just hoped Mom and Dad would see it the same way.

After finally getting a few hours of sleep, I woke up the next morning and went downstairs to find Megan sitting by herself with a cup of coffee at the kitchen island bar.

"Where's Mom and Dad?" I asked.

"Check this out." She pushed a note in Mom's handwriting across the bar to me.

I slid onto the stool next to her and read it.

Dad and I need some time away to talk some more. We're going up to the state park for some alone time. Will be back tonight.

We love you,

Mom and Dad

"Dang," they've run away!" I exclaimed.

"They haven't run away, you dufus," she chided, pulling the note back across the bar. "It just says they need a little time away. I can certainly understand that."

"They sure did plenty of talking last night," I said reaching for the box of Cheerios and a bowl. 'Course I couldn't understand what they were saying, but it kept me awake. Kinda sounded like they were arguing."

"Mom and Dad hardly ever argue," Megan said.

"So, what do you think?" I asked.

"About what?"

"About Grampa, you dufus." I grinned.

"Okay, sorry about calling you a dufus, but I am kinda mad at you."

"Why?" I said, reaching for the milk and watching it flow into the bowl, floating my Cheerios.

"Because you were having so much fun and excitement doing all that time travel without sharing anything about it with your loving sister. You gotta tell me all about it."

"I will, but tell me, do you believe everything Grampa said?"

"Why not? After everything he showed us, there's no way not to believe him. You believe him, don't you? I mean about the bad guys and saving the world and all that."

"Yeah, for sure," I said around a mouthful of Cheerios. "He wouldn't be going to all that trouble otherwise. You know it had to cost him a fortune to build that big bunker downstairs. Then he put that equipment in, and hired those specialists to find and protect all that stuff. He wouldn't be doing that without a really good reason.

"I guess if we could help him find something that should be protected from the bad guys, it would be a good thing. I don't know if I could ever think of myself as someone that could save the world, though."

"Yeah," she said leaning back on her stool, looking me up and down. "Superheroes usually have more meat on their bones," She giggled. "You'd better start bulking up before you start shopping for a pair of tights and a cape."

"So, I guess *you're* a regular Wonder Woman, huh?"

"Well actually," she made a move like she was fluffing her hair and said haughtily, "I was thinking my new title should be something like Princess of Discovery—no, make that, *Goddess* of Discovery. But since you're my little brother, you can simply call me, Goddess—or Your Highness."

"Oh my gosh," I rolled my eyes. "What have we created? Come on, get serious, now," I said, trying to turn my sister's silliness into something more critical to us at the moment. "How do you think Mom and Dad will handle this whole thing with Grampa? It's obvious what they needed to get away from us to talk about."

"I don't know," she said, returning from her world of make-believe. "I'm sure they're just being protective. There's a lot to digest; all this time travel, find and save the documents, bad guys, rooms full of workers, treasures in the basement, and save the world stuff. I'm surprised Mom and Dad aren't planning to be gone for a week or more. You know they just want the best for us."

I slid the cereal bowl aside. "Yeah, but there's still a lot of unknowns for us. I mean the family. You know, Grampa said you and I, and even Mom could be changing—getting smarter."

"That can't be a bad thing. Right?" She smiled. "I think a little extra boost for the rest of high school and college would be good, don't you?"

"Sure," I said. "I'll take all the help I can get, but still, I can't help but be concerned. We'll all learn things we wouldn't have known otherwise. Things will just be different. Will Dad be left out while you, I, and Mom are changing and learning new things?"

"No, Max. It won't have to be that way. We can all keep him informed. You know, families grow and change all the time. We changed from babies to little kids to big kids to teenagers. Mom and Dad changed with us. We all changed together. It could be the same, as we get into helping Grampa with his projects. We can all share our experiences with each other, especially Dad. You know how much he loves history. I think this whole thing will strengthen our family."

"I just hope that Mom and Dad will see it that way and ask for our input," I said.

Rather than hang around all day waiting and wondering about what decision Mom and Dad would make, I called the guys and invited them over to shag a few balls and watch the Sunday afternoon baseball game on TV. The Rangers were playing the Yankees. Should be a good game. I checked in the fridge and pantry and found enough stuff to make sandwiches, chips and dip, and sodas.

I'd been a Texas Rangers baseball fan as long as I could remember. Every season Dad usually took the whole family to at least one game, sometimes two. He also gets tickets once a year for just the two of us for a guy's night out and we drive up to Arlington for a game with all the baseball park food we can stand.

Megan isn't the biggest baseball fan, but she doesn't get left out. Mom always takes her once a year during the summer to one of the big malls in Dallas or Fort Worth for shopping and they usually go to a concert or show afterward. So, we both get our turn for a special day with a parent.

The game on TV was a good one, with the lead changing a couple of times in the late innings. For some weird reason, Rick was a Yankees fan and loved to wear his Yankees baseball cap just to irritate Jeremy and me. Of course, we enjoyed ribbing him whenever the Yankees made a bonehead mistake or the Rangers made a good play. So, it was always a fun time of trash talk whenever a Rangers/Yankees game was on TV and the guys were over watching it with me. We sat on the floor in the den, around the coffee table loaded with what was left of the snacks. I wore my red Rangers T-shirt, Jeremy had his blue Rangers cap on, and Rick sported his well-worn black Yankees cap.

It was the beginning of the bottom of the ninth when Mom and Dad pulled into the driveway. After saying hello to the guys, Mom headed upstairs to see what Megan was doing and Dad joined us in the den to watch the last inning.

"Hi guys," Dad said. "Been listening to it on the car radio. Pretty good game huh?"

"Yeah, looks like my Yanks are gonna pull off another win," Rick said.

"Don't be too sure of that," I said. "We've got some power hitters coming up."

The Rangers were behind going into the bottom of the ninth but pulled off a big, exciting win with a double with men on second and third. Of course, Rick did all his what-ifs, and they coulda, and they shoulda excuses.

But I said, "hey man, what counts is what's on the scoreboard at the end of the game."

"Yeah, yeah, yeah," Rick said as he and Jeremy gathered their gloves and headed for the door.

"Well," Dad said, "maybe your Yanks will win it next time."

"You mean the division or the World Series?" Rick grinned over his shoulder.

"How about just the next game. They won't be playing the Rangers," Dad answered, laughing.

"Hey man, thanks for the snacks," Jeremy said, casually poking Rick and nodding toward the table loaded with leftover snacks.

"Oh, yeah, thanks. That was good," Rick said, remembering his manners with Jeremy's help.

CHAPTER 17

"I'm glad to see you had your friends over to watch the game today," Dad said closing the door behind the guys. "They're both good boys, aren't they?"

"I guess they are," I said. "Jeremy's always been a straight arrow, and although Rick's a little goofy at times, he's really a good guy."

"So, are you and Mom okay?" My directness surprised even me, but I was worried about them.

"Your Mom and me? Of course, we're okay." Dad smiled and patted me on the shoulder. You know, after everything that happened yesterday at your grandfather's, there was just a lot for us to talk over, just the two of us. So, we got away for a few hours. That's all. We talked it all out, and now, we need to sit down with you and your sister and have a family meeting. Are you okay with that?"

"I was hoping we would. When? Now?"

"Yes, let me go get them and bring them down here. Looks like you have a few sandwiches left over. That can be our dinner."

While Dad went upstairs to get Mom and Megan, I moved the tray of chips and dip to the kitchen and added more to the tray. I also sat out fresh bread and the leftover tuna salad from the fridge in case we needed more sandwiches. I also poured sodas for everyone.

Soon, we were all sitting around the kitchen table with Megan and me waiting and wondering what would happen.

Dad started the discussion. "I think we all know what's been on all of our minds since yesterday. Your grandfather came into our lives and all of a sudden, we've been presented with all kinds of wild and bizarre stuff. We've been confronted with things like extreme magic, time travel adventures, ancient discoveries, scientific advancements beyond our time, supervillains, and our children with potential to save the world. If that's not wild and bizarre, I don't know what is.

"As you know, I was pretty skeptical—in the beginning. But I've been convinced with everything I've seen and heard. All that appears to be impossible is actually true. I don't know how it can be, but it is. I'm now a believer. I know how your mother feels. We've talked at length about it and she agrees with me. So, how do you two feel about it? Do you believe what your grandfather said yesterday? Do you believe all of it?"

I looked at Megan to hear her response.

"How could I not be," she said. "Of course, I've not experienced the time travel adventures as much as Max, but I know what happened to me. They weren't dreams. I was there, in another time, watching the world through the eyes of another person. I transitioned there and back in a very calm, comfortable way. I felt absolutely safe through the whole process. Then with everything Grampa showed us last night, I thoroughly understand and buy into what he's doing and why. Dad, he's doing the right thing for all the right reasons. He's dedicated his life to it." She turned to me to hear what I had to say.

"I agree with her," I said. "Yes, I've done more trips into the past than her, and I understand why Grampa wanted to explain things to you himself, rather than me. He explained things much better than I ever could. And yes, I know Grampa is truthful with all of us. We're family. He wants to share his life with us. He's taken on a really big job. He just wants his family to be a part of it and see that it continues after he's gone. It could all be lost if we don't join him. We're the only family he has."

The room was quiet for a moment until Mom spoke up. "Okay, now that we know we are all in agreement about who and what your grandfather is, what he does, and what he wants of us, and is offering us, what are we going to do with it? The way I see it, we have two choices:

"We can continue with our life as it is without participating in your grandfather's world. We have a good life. We are a close-knit, happy family. We have a positive value system and work hard together to achieve our realistic goals. Your dad and I are proud of both of you. We believe you'll have a good future following your dreams through college and on through life without taking part in your Grandfather's plan for us. In other words, we could just continue being the regular American family that we are without magic and time travel and all of that. We can still love and maintain our relationship with your grampa, but just without all his *baggage*, if you will."

She hesitated and took a deep breath before continuing. "Then, on the other hand, we, as a family, can choose to follow your grandfather's plan. We've seen evidence through Max and his grades that becoming involved in Papa's magic and power will give you a boost in your drive, focus, and intellectual ability. That could have a tremendous positive impact on both of your personal successes through your entire lives.

"We also know how important it is to help find and protect those critical lost documents. We don't know at this point, just how we could fit in with the protecting part, but we're willing to learn. We also know how much fun *and* how educational his adventures can be. Another thing to consider is the time required to conduct the missions for your grandfather. It will take zero amount of your time because you will be asleep while your tasks are being done. Therefore, you can go about your life as usual. It shouldn't interrupt your school, social life, college studies, or your life afterward. But, I guess, the most positive aspect of following your grampa's plan is that you could indeed have an impact on keeping the world safe.

"Now, I think you'll agree that your dad and I have never tried to dictate how you live your lives. We've tried to give you positive guidance that will help you make good decisions for you and your life. You've done that. You've chosen good friends. You've avoided bad habits, and you have a good moral base. One of the hardest decisions any parent can make is learning how much and when to let go at the right times.

"So, with the understanding that we believe you are both mature enough to be a part of this decision, we want you to get together and decide what you both agree to do. We will do this as a family. Your father and I have decided that we will support whatever decision you make. We can accept going either way.

Understand also that if at any time you realize that you've made a mistake, your decision can be reversed. Any questions?"

I looked at Megan. "Do we need a meeting to decide?"

"I don't think so," she said, grinning. "You know what I want to do."

"The Goddess of Discovery and I want to be a part of the Discovery Corps," I said with conviction. "When can we tell Grampa?"

CHAPTER 18

Mom called Grampa the next morning and invited him over for dinner that evening. Mom, Megan and I were nervous with anticipation, going through our regular activities, waiting for the day to pass, Dad to come home from work, and Grampa to come over for dinner.

He rang the doorbell at precisely 7:00 as invited. He was neatly attired in casual slacks, navy-blue sports coat, and open-collared shirt. We managed small talk for a few minutes while Megan and I served Mom, Dad, and Grampa wine.

Dad had earlier told Megan and me not to put the salmon on the grill until he said to. So, we poured ourselves sodas and joined Grampa, Mom, and Dad in the den. Once we were all seated, Dad started the conversation.

"We all know why we're here, so I see no point dragging things out." He turned to Grampa. "Sir, after hours of deliberation between Susan and I, and with the total agreement of Max and Megan, we've decided that our family will join you and support the goals and efforts of the House of Discovery. The kids are both excited about what journeys they can take to help you uncover more secrets of the past. And Susan wants to ease slowly into your operation at first by just peeking into the lives of some famous people and events of the past. Not to be left out, I want to be of assistance however I can to help with the operation. So, we're all diving in head first into the world of time travel, historical research and discovery. We don't know at this point to what extent our lives will change, but we're all up for the journey." His grin was infectious as he looked around the room.

Grampa bounced up from his chair almost like a teenager and rushed over to embrace, Dad, Megan, me and Mom. "You don't know how happy this makes me." When he pulled away from Mom, he brushed tears from his eyes. "I don't know why I'm so emotional," he said, "this is a celebration."

"It sure is, Dad said. "I'll be right back." He headed into the kitchen, leaving us standing, and returned briefly with a bottle of chilled Champagne in one hand and glasses in the other. He unwrapped the foil covering the cork and worked the cork with his thumbs until it popped out. As he poured, he said, "I believe our family lived a pretty normal, maybe even a little boring, existence going about our regular routine—work and school, chores around the house, and social activities. We did some fun things to break the day-to-day pattern, like camping and taking little vacations and such, but I can see that now everything can change in an unbelievably exciting and adventurous way. What you've offered the kids and Susan is the opportunity of a lifetime. They'll learn things they could never learn otherwise. How can I refuse my family all of that?

"Here, let's have a toast." He held his glass high, as we all reached for ours. Dad waited till we all joined him with our glasses in the air.

"To Doctor Magas and his wonderful magic. He's brought magnificent adventure and discovery to this family. We're so happy that we finally found each other!" We touched our glasses and drank.

Grampa's eyes were wet again, but he wanted to say something too.

"You're right Tom; Megan and Max will learn a good amount of history with us at the House of Discovery. They'll participate in exciting events in the past, but they'll still need a well-rounded and in-depth education that only a good university and graduate school can provide.

"I've been lucky enough to be in a position to help see that they can get the best education possible. Educational trusts have been established for both of them. Those trust will provide whatever costs are necessary to universities of your choosing. There is no doubt in my mind that they will easily qualify for admission. Their futures will be challenging, and they must be prepared for whatever comes their way."

"Mom fell into Grampa's arms. "Oh, Papa!" The sounds barely escaped her lips. "Are you serious?"

"Very serious, my dear." A gentle smile covered Grampa's face as Megan, Dad, and I all crowded in to embrace and thank our grandfather.

"How did you know which direction we would take with this," Dad asked after shaking Grampa's hand in gratitude.

"I didn't," Grampa laughed. "I'm a magician, not a mind reader. For all I knew, you might have said you didn't want anything to do with The House of Discovery. Obviously, I'm glad it didn't turn out that way."

"But you went ahead and set up an educational fund for them anyway"

"Of course. They're my grandchildren. I'm just glad I found them in time to help out.

"Tom, I don't mean to take anything away from you and Susan in what you've been doing to prepare for their educational costs, but I know everything's very expensive these days, and none of you should have to worry about those expenses when I can help out."

"Thank you, sir. I just hope they make you as proud of them as Susan and I are." Dad gave Megan and me a wink.

"I'm already very proud of them," Grampa said, looking at us. Megan and I were still hanging onto him.

"So, let's see if they can give us something else tonight to be proud of," Dad said. "Hey guys, go ahead and start the dinner on the grill. I don't know about anybody else, but all this excitement has made me hungry."

Megan planted a kiss on Grampa's cheek as we headed for the patio. "Thanks again, Grampa."

CHAPTER 19

Soon we were seated around the patio table. Overhead fans kept the air moving and created a slight summer breeze. Megan and I had decorated with TIKI torches along the edges of the patio and a couple of candles on the table and the outdoor bar.

The thick salmon steaks turned out moist, flaky and flavorful. They were served over a bed of rice with grilled squash, asparagus and red bell peppers for color alongside the rice. Megan drizzled her warm special sauce over the salmon and rice just after I delivered each plate.

"You kids have outdone yourselves again with the dinner," Grampa said between bites.

"Thanks," I said. "Megan and I both enjoy cooking and Mom and Dad encourage it. We're learning a lot."

"They can keep me challenged to keep up with their requests for special ingredients," Mom said. "Sometimes we just keep it simple though with burgers or sandwiches."

Grampa changed the subject. "There's more we need to discuss. Megan and Susan, have you thought any more about who, where and when you'd like to visit? You know you have some catching up to do with Max and the adventures he's taken."

Mom answered, "I was thinking just today how wonderful it would be to see Princess Diana's wedding from her point of view." She grinned at Megan. "That was like a fairytale wedding. Wouldn't that be special?"

"Yeah, I'd like to see that too, but what I think would be really fun would be going to visit Cleopatra during her time and place. That would be so cool."

"Okay, Grampa said, Cleopatra and Princess Di it is. I'll make the arrangements."

Grampa looked across the table at Dad. "Tom, you're a very generous man to give your family these opportunities without any expectations for yourself."

Dad smiled. "It would be nice to be able to do the time travel adventures with them, but I know that can't happen, so I'll be happy to hear about them from Susan and the kids. You know, I've always been interested in history, and I'm sure the stories about their experiences will bring them to life for me."

Grampa ran his fingers through his beard, smoothing the whiskers. "You know, Tom, much of our business has to do with all kinds of research. When I first met the family, I wanted to know more about you, so I looked you up on the internet. Hope you don't mind. Just innocent curiosity, I guess. I was pleasantly surprised at how much your name popped up in general searches about your line of work. When we first met, you told me you worked at a local office of a large company that does computer services for corporations all over the world. Seems like you're a very accomplished and well-respected guy in your industry. New software development here, total software and hardware integration projects there, a good deal of security systems development, even some patent applications. Quite a broad scope of work. You couldn't have accomplished everything you've done without doing a lot of deep research. You're a very impressive guy.

"Tom, you've got the kind of skills I've been hoping to add to our team at the House of Discovery. Why don't you come by one evening this week after your work so we can discuss some details of how you could become an integral part of the House of Discovery? How does—uh, tomorrow sound to you? I'll ask Jeffery to plan a dinner for just the two of us."

My jaw dropped as I shared glances between Mom and Megan.

Dad couldn't hide his surprise at the compliments and the unexpected job opportunity. "Why, sure, I'd be happy to. I'll look forward to it. Would six o'clock tomorrow be okay?" His face flushed behind his grin.

"It would be perfect," Grampa said. His eyes twinkled and his lips parted into his own smile, widening his beard as he looked over the rim of his wine glass.

"Oh," Grampa continued, "since we're discussing jobs, Max, Megan, and Susan, when you decide you're ready to spread your wings beyond, what we'll call, 'time travel tourism,' and want to do actual research missions, you'll be paid accordingly. How about fifty dollars per each mission to start? As the missions get more complex, they'll obviously be worth more. Does that sound fair?"

Megan answered as her eyes widened with her smile, "You mean you want to pay us for sleeping?"

"That's precisely what I mean, but you'll have things to do for me while on your missions. For example, you'll be given a list of things to look for beforehand, and I'd expect at least a verbal report of your findings after the completion of the mission. Is that fair enough?"

"That's more than generous, Papa," Mom said. "Actually, I can't speak for the kids, but I'd do it for free. We'd be sleeping, for heaven's sake!"

"Yes," Grampa said, "your body will be sleeping, but your subconscious will have important things to do—information to collect. So, awake, or asleep, you'll be paid. Besides, young people have things they need money for. Right guys? But we'll deal with all that later. For now, I want you to just enjoy yourselves, become comfortable with the travel process and have a good time as you learn about the world before your time.

"Since Max is a bit ahead of you and Megan with his experience, he's ready to take on actual assignments. We can start with you, Max, anytime."

"Bring it on," I said, grinning, and reached over to fist bump Grampa. "I'm ready!"

CHAPTER 20

I wasn't kidding when I said I was ready to go. By mid-morning, the next day, I was sitting in the recreation room in Grampa's bunker. Grampa sat across the table from me.

"So," I said, "what's this new role I'll be taking on?"

"It means for each journey that you take, you'll have a targeted host that we're researching. Perhaps, your assignment may take you to several different times or events in your host's life, but it will still only require a relative flash in your physical time— always, of course, while you're asleep. All other aspects of your journey will be the same as what you've experienced before. The only difference between your new assignment and the journeys you've been taking is that you'll know in advance who your target host will be and you'll look for specific things.

"It also means that from time to time as you mature and get more experience with the whole program, you may take on research assignments to do the developmental work like the rest of the team, seeking information about targets from history that may have lost discoveries we're trying to find. We'll also eventually get you involved with the archeologists to help unearth treasures when we pinpoint their locations with our investigations.

"You see, Max, our team is constantly searching any resource available on the lives and accomplishments of certain individuals who made significant contributions to science, medicine, and the arts—things that enhanced the human experience. We look for more than just my ancestors who may have been scientists. We look for people with creative minds; those who experimented to improve what they knew and made it better.

Our people seek what may appear to be the most insignificant bits of information about a person, and dig around them to see if they can find evidence that may lead to their accomplishments that were not made public during their lifetime.

"Then after they exhaust all their leads and document their findings, they turn the file over to me—now us." He smiled and winked at me. "That's when we'll actually go nose around with that person in their time and place to see what, if anything, they might have left behind that, if further developed, could lead to new and exciting discoveries. Many of them *are* scientific breakthroughs. Occasionally we also find exquisite works of art that were hidden away and forgotten over time, like those you saw in the vault."

"There must be dozens of people like that from all through the ages to investigate," I said.

"Oh, more like hundreds, perhaps thousands," he said. "There are many who did their work in the shadows, without fanfare. Who knows how many important scientific discoveries or near breakthroughs never saw the light of day?

"So, with that, let's get down to business." He tapped a file of documents in front of him with his finger. "This is the file the crew put together on Doctor McAllister. Let's go back to him. He's the man you became familiar with during the Lewis and Clark Expedition. You only saw a small snippet of his life then. He was a very interesting man with an exciting life. As a young man, when you first visited him, he was actually more an adventurer than a man of science. All that came later. You saw how he got involved with the study of plants used for healing while with Lewis and Clark."

"Yeah," I said, nodding. "He learned a lot and took a whole bunch of notes."

"We know," Grampa agreed. "All those notes and journals survived that long trip to the Pacific Ocean and back. He stored them in a safe place in St. Louis upon his return for more thorough study.

"By then he had the bug for adventure and was learning all he could about Native American healing methods with plants. So much so that he made several more trips over the years into the unknown parts of the west with other adventurers.

"The most notable of these was Jedediah Smith, the famous Indian fighter, fur trapper, and explorer. Your next journey will be to become a part of Jake McAllister when he joins Jedediah Smith and his men as they go about their fur trapping and mapping expeditions in the western United States."

"Wow, that sounds like fun. What do you want me to look for?"

"We especially want to know if he is documenting his finds as he did with the Lewis and Clark expedition. If so, how does he keep his documents safe, and does he always keep them with him? Also, make note of any healing or medical treatment he does with the men in his group or to any of the Indians they encounter."

"Okay, that doesn't sound too hard," I said, nodding.

Grampa looked me in the eyes and lifted his forefinger toward me. "Now, the last thing I'll ask you to do sounds a little strange, but it's important."

"What's that?"

"Look for anyone you run across that may appear to be out of place, like perhaps he doesn't belong."

"In what way?" I was confused.

"Maybe his clothing doesn't seem to blend naturally with what the others are wearing. Look for subtle things. I doubt if anything would be a glaring difference. Look for strange behavior. Perhaps someone seems to be asking a lot of questions, especially about plants and cures."

"Why do you think someone like that would be with the group?" Then it occurred to me. I drew a quick breath, my voice almost caught in my throat. "Do you think the bad guys are sending out spies?" I said breathlessly.

Grampa lifted his bushy eyebrows and looked over the tops of his glasses. "You're catching on fast," he said. "Our investigation has given us an indication that Doctor Volkov has also developed an interest in the life of Doctor McAllister and may be looking into his background."

"Wait a minute," I said. Who's this Doctor Volkov? Is he one of the bad guys?"

Grampa hesitated a moment to gather his thoughts. "You know Max, I've gotten ahead of myself. Let's back up some and I'll explain. This is important.

"You see, our ancestors and their magical power go back hundreds of years, maybe even thousands. During those centuries, they've produced thousands of offspring who've scattered to every corner of the world.

"Most lines of descent lost those magical powers altogether ages ago. But of those family lines that worked to maintain, develop, and strengthen their magic, only a handful remain today. We are one of those lines.

"Those of us today that retained their magic have used it, for the most part, in quiet and positive ways. Some used their enhanced ability to learn and increase their intellect to become the very best in their field. Some became wonderful composers, musicians, and talented artists. Others excelled in fields such as business, trade, transportation, or construction. Still, others found far-reaching success in medicine and the sciences. I used mine to support my efforts in the study of science and historical and archeological research.

"However, in any large group of people, there are always some that take the dark side. I've learned that at least one of my very distant relatives is practicing a modern-day version of dark magic. There could be others."

"What's dark magic?" I asked.

Grampa looked at me, then got a far away, icy look in his eyes. He hesitated a moment, then whispered. "It's evil, Max. It's very evil."

My eyes widened and the hair on the back of my neck stood up before I asked, "What do those dark magic guys do?"

He was silent again briefly, apparently searching for a way to explain.

"Essentially, they use supernatural powers for evil and very selfish purposes. Some of them have been associated with devil worship, voodoo, hexes, curses and much worse."

"So, this dark magic guy is the enemy?" I asked"

"Yes, his name is Doctor Volkov. He grew up in Eastern Europe, but now he's here in this country. He's ruthless in his greed and will stop at nothing to get what he wants."

"What *does* he want?"

"Essentially, anything that will give him power and the riches that go with it. What he really wants are secret documents similar to what we protect here at The House of Discovery. Some treasures like that could be sold to the highest bidder to be used for evil purposes, and he could become one of the richest and most powerful people in the world.

"You see, he's also developed very strong magic over the years, but not to the level that I have. He learned of my work some time ago and has been trying to duplicate what I do; seeking information from the past and recovering priceless lost records. So far, he's not been successful. I've been able to foil him by staying ahead of him with every project.

"He's uncovered a method of time travel, but he accomplishes it in a totally different way than I. His methods are clumsy, crude, and sometimes dangerous. He uses an awkward body transport method that is supposed to move a physical person from current times to a particular place in history and back. From what our research indicates, he's had some accidents, missing his target location and times, both coming and going. He sends people into the past, in their own living flesh—or attempts to anyway. They're out of place, and trespassing into the past, one might say. I'm sure you would spot it if one of his associates were where you were. If that's the case, just keep an eye on them and report back what you see. Understand?"

"Yes, sir."

"So, your next adventure will be with Jake McAllister on the Jedediah Smith expedition. One of the chapters in the book you have and your bookmark will get you where you need to be. Enjoy!"

"Yes, sir." A whim of silliness overcame me as I rose from the table, stood at attention, saluted my grandfather, and said sharply, "Discovery Cadet Max Malone is on assignment, sir."

Grampa rolled his eyes and gave me a silly salute in return as he got up from the table to escort me back upstairs. He draped his arm over my shoulder as we headed toward the hallway. "We don't normally salute here, and titles aren't necessary, but if you want one, we'll have to come up with one a little impressive than 'Discovery Cadet'. How about 'Captain Discovery'?"

"Hey, that sounds good to me. Wait till you hear what Megan's calling herself."

CHAPTER 21

My next assignment sounded exciting, but there was something else going on that evening that was thrilling for the whole family. Mom, Megan and I were waiting for Dad to get home from his meeting with Grampa. Since Dad was having dinner at Grampa's place, we had dinner without him but saved dessert for when he got home. He and Grampa were talking about Dad actually going to work for the House of Discovery. Wow! Wouldn't that be cool? We could *all* be doing stuff for Grampa and his discovery projects.

We brewed a fresh pot of decaf coffee to have with the pie and ice cream later. Finally, at about nine o'clock, we heard his car pull into the garage.

"Hi," he said, coming through the door. His face told nothing about what had gone on for the past three hours. He walked past me and Megan sitting on stools at the counter, opened the fridge door and took out a beer. He wasn't making eye contact with any of us. He popped the cap and tilted it to his lips.

Mom stood next to the breakfast table. "Well?" she said, tilting her head forward with not only a question in her voice but also on her face and body. Her shoulders were hunched, and her hands were outstretched, palms upward, waiting for his response.

"Well—what?" he said after swallowing the sip of beer. His expression revealed nothing.

"Mom let out a sigh of exasperation. "Your meeting with Papa—that's what."

"Oh that. We had a nice chat." He reached for the stack of mail on the corner of the counter island and started sorting through it.

"Thomas Edward Malone," Mom said in *that* voice. She grabbed the mail from his hand and put it back on the counter. "You quit playing with us and give us an answer." She was trying to sound angry, but it wasn't working. Her eyes and the edges of her mouth were betraying her efforts to scold Dad.

Dad couldn't maintain his straight face any longer. A big smile crossed his face as he pulled Mom to him in a big hug. "Let's talk about it over coffee. I think I smell a fresh pot." That was Megan's cue to cut and plate the apple pie and pop them in the microwave to warm them up. While she did that, I poured the coffee and got the ice cream ready to spoon on the pieces of warm pie. Mom continued to pump Dad for details of the meeting to no avail.

Soon we all sat around the closeness of the breakfast table with dessert and coffee to talk about Dad's future.

"I'll ask you again," Mom said playfully, "tell us what happened."

Dad took a sip of coffee. "Your father and I had a nice dinner while he told me about the requirements and expectations of the job. It seems like I have the skills and experience needed.

"The primary expectations are to do what everybody else does—find evidence that could lead to hidden documents and treasure. Sometimes, though, a lot of effort goes down the drain with nothing found. Travel is occasionally required to track down information that just isn't available via the internet.

"There are also software and hardware upgrades that need to be designed and developed that will enhance the searches. There's plenty to be done."

He continued. "After we talked about the details of the job, and the goals of the organization, I had the opportunity to meet and have a good question and answer session with each of the team members. What a super bunch of professionals they are. They all love it there and really enjoy the flexibility of their jobs.

"After the team and I finished interviewing each other, Doctor Magas left me alone in the recreation room with the huge TV so he could have a follow-up discussion with the team.

"When he returned, he said I made a positive impression on the team. Then he went into all the benefits of the job. By then I had a good feeling that he was going to make me a firm offer."

Dad took another sip of coffee and a sizable bite of pie and ice cream. The table was silent while we watched him chew. "Mmm, good pie," he said, and started to take another bite.

"Don't. You. Dare take another bite of that pie until you tell us." Mom upped the intensity on *that* voice.

"Tell you what?" Dad tried to put on his innocent face again. It didn't work so well.

No words were necessary from Mom because of the glare she gave Dad. It was *that* glare, which was even worse than *that* voice.

Megan and I were in stitches. Seldom had we seen Mom and Dad go through such a comedy routine in front of us.

Finally, Dad couldn't hold back anymore. "Yes, I got the offer," he blurted, "and yes, it's a great offer, and yes, the working conditions, salary, and benefits are much better than my current job, and yes, I'll accept it—if my family agrees."

"You mean you didn't tell him yes?" Mom said wide-eyed.

"No. The offer will still be good tomorrow. Just thought I should bounce it all off you guys first."

"I think you should take it," I said. "I think it will be cool working with you. I plan on being there a lot."

Of course, Megan and Mom agreed with me. Dad said he would give his notice to resign his old job the next day and would be working full time with Grampa in about two weeks.

Our celebration lasted for another hour as we talked about our future with Grampa's House of Discovery. Megan and Mom shared their hopes of visiting exotic places and people throughout history, and Dad talked about a few of the exciting research projects Grampa had planned for the future. I was thrilled to have my whole family now involved in the exhilarating world of time travel adventure. I could talk freely among them about my experiences and enjoy theirs with them. It was a perfect day.

CHAPTER 22

I couldn't think of a better way to top off such a perfect day than to take on my next assignment. I climbed the stairs to my room, looking forward to whatever the next journey would bring. The big book on my bedside table caught my attention as I entered. I sat on the edge of my bed and rested my hand on its cover for a moment to feel it's welcoming glow. I had become used to the warm feeling of the book and the faint, barely noticeable vibration it emitted when I touched it. I think it was the book's way of telling me that it was prepared to send me on another exciting adventure.

Soon I was ready for bed and slid under the covers on my belly with the big book opened under my chin. I found the chapter about Jedediah Smith, placed the bookmarker between the pages and started reading.

Jedediah Smith—Mountain Man

Jedediah Smith (1798-1831) was a trapper author, map maker, explorer and Indian fighter of whom legends are made. The twenty-four-year-old adventurer responded to a newspaper advertisement for "One Hundred Enterprising Young Men" to explore and trap fur in the Rocky Mountains. Smith's six-foot-tall commanding presence impressed the owner of the company to hire him. He soon found himself with a large crew rowing up the Missouri river on the keelboat, *Enterprise*, starting his first adventure as a mountain man

It was a successful campaign lasting well over a year that taught Smith not only the skill of fur trapping but the bold ways of the mountain man and a good knowledge of the Native American tribes of the West. It also fueled a pursuit for knowledge and adventure that brought him to lead several more campaigns to explore where no white man had been, trap for fur and document maps for much of the Rocky Mountains, southwestern desert, and the Pacific coastal regions. Smith's explorations and documented travels were important resources to later American westward expansion.

The beginning of my transition again came as no surprise. I knew what to expect and soon was undergoing the process. After separating from my physical body, my spirit, as I'm beginning to call it, started on its journey back in time. I always enjoyed the trip to my destination because of the visions of different periods of history I see during the time regression. Soon the trip was coming to an end and my spirit was shifting into my host's body.

I was again a part of the familiar body of Jake McAllister. I was knee-deep in water, setting a beaver trap next one of the entrances leading into the jumbled branches of a beaver dam. Of course, I was not the same young Jake that I was during the Lewis and Clark Expedition. I was twenty years older with lots more experience than I had then.

This was my third expedition to the Northwest since the Lewis and Clark trek. In the meantime, I'd studied medicine and became a doctor. I enjoyed practicing medicine, but my heart was with my research and the adventure that came with it.

Our leader, Jedediah Smith was a respected, veteran mountain man despite his youth. He was not yet thirty years old. He had proven himself in previous expeditions as a bold adventurer, fearless Indian fighter, and mapmaker of previously uncharted territories. He carried a reputation in the fur trade as a dependable producer of fine pelts.

Our company was made of a good mix of men. All had hunting and trapping experience from growing up on family farms. But only a handful had the experience of a mountain man who spent months in all kinds of weather, working sometimes in waist-deep water setting traps and retrieving beaver, and tracking other animals for food and fur. Few had the experience of traveling hundreds, if not thousands of miles by boat, canoe, horseback, snowshoe, or by foot through all types of terrain and hazards to collect fur for a demanding world-wide market. A recent Indian fight was a stark realization of just how fragile life could be in the wild country ruled by Indians and animals at the top of the food chain.

We were trapping and moving west along one of the east-west tributaries that led to the Missouri River. We were a company of only twenty-nine men. We lost six men in the Indian fight a few weeks earlier when a trade deal for buffalo robes went bad at the

Arikara village about a hundred miles downstream. Three other men received serious injuries in the battle.

I'd had little time to pursue my passion for collecting and documenting plant specimens since the Indian encounter. My evenings were filled tending the wounded after a full day of traveling or trapping. They were making good progress toward recovery. Much of the success of their treatment, I believe, was due to the use of the concoctions I made from my collection. Up to that point, I had collected, documented and cataloged a good number of plants, roots, and berries for my research, enough to require a separate horse to carry the specimens and documentation.

It was one of those nights when the stranger walked into camp. The sun had just gone down on that crisp, autumn evening when the man, a white man, emerged from the darkening woods and walked into our camp.

"Hello the camp," he called from the edge of the clearing. "The meat roasting over the fire smells good," he said, continuing to walk toward the encampment. He spoke with a pronounced accent. It sounded eastern European.

It wasn't terribly unusual to encounter people on the frontier with a European accent. There were many French trappers working in the French companies to the north. America was a country of immigrants, so several of the men in our company spoke English with distinctive British, Irish, Scottish, and even Polish and Russian accents.

We were startled by the sounds of encroachment from the edge of the clearing. Each man reached for his rifle, which was never more than an arms-reach away.

"Who goes there!" Jedediah Smith called, leveling his rifle toward the man.

"I am a friend," the stranger answered. He stopped, leaned over and put his rifle on the ground. Standing back up, he raised his arms in the air to show his hands were empty. "I mean you no harm. Allow me to come to your fire and I will introduce myself."

Smith hesitated a moment before answering while he sized up the man standing sixty paces beyond his rifle's sight. The man was alone and afoot, carrying nothing more than a rifle, a rolled-up blanket, and a pack on his back. "Come on in," Smith said. He lowered the rifle, but still kept an eye on the man as he picked up his weapon and resumed his walk toward the fire.

What a strange sight he was, alone and without a horse. Everyone stopped what they were doing to watch the man walk into camp. He was tall and slender. He wore ill-fitting dark wool pants and coat, and leather boots. A powder horn hung from his shoulder and a leather bag, probably loaded with lead bullets hung from his belt. He wore a large knife in a leather sheath on the other side of his body from the bullet bag. A black slouch hat concealed most of the man's dark hair.

As he got closer to the fire, I found his facial features interesting. He had a narrow, beaked nose and deep-set dark eyes. His high cheekbones accented his hollow cheeks. The most notable feature about his face, though, was his beard. He hardly had any. He wore less than a week's worth of beard growth. The men that I worked and traveled with, without exception, wore full beards for the duration of our expedition. Some had thicker beards than others, but most were grown rather long. It kept the flies and mosquitoes off our faces in the summer and helped keep us warm in the winter.

I was finishing changing the dressings of the men I was caring for and watched the stranger as he approached the fire. Several men, including Smith, were already there.

"My name is Edward," the tall man said as he dropped his gear. "I'm happy to find you." He bowed slightly at the waist. He looked back and forth between the men and the deer roasting on a spit over the flames. "I was separated from a French trapping company three weeks ago and been lost ever since. Who do I have the pleasure of meeting?" He was using his best English to impress, but his thick accent made his English sound rough.

"My name's Jedediah Smith. This is my trapping company. Don't you have a horse?"

"The French took him when they left me to die."

"Can't imagine they wanted you dead if they left you with your rifle, your shooting gear, and your kit," Smith said.

"That's what happened. Is the deer done?" He said, changing the subject"

Edward made himself at home around the campsite that night. After eating his fill of supper, he started circulating around the camp meeting the men and talking with them as they finished their chores for the day. Some were skinning their catch by firelight. Others were making frames and stretching the hides to dry. A few were repairing traps or cleaning and oiling their weapons before bedtime.

After dinner, I sat close to the fire bringing my documentation up to date regarding the specimens I'd found the last few days while I followed the trap line. I was about to put my journals away when Edward came and sat beside me.

"I have not met you. Who are you?" he said straightforwardly. I was still trying to figure out his accent. It sounded Russian, or maybe Polish.

Jacob McAlister," I said. I'm the company doctor among other things." I couldn't help but notice a little twitch in his face and a slight smile when he heard my name.

"You do much writing," he said looking over the stack of journals I was organizing to load into their waterproof bag.

"Yes, I suppose I do."

"Many books. What do you put in so many books?"

"Oh, I just note things I find as I go about my work."

"What kinds of things?"

"You know, Edward, it's getting late and I need to check my patients once again before I turn in. I'm sure we'll get better acquainted another day." I finished shoving my documents into their bag, secured the closure and took it to my bedroll and other gear before looking in on the recovering men.

Later, under my blankets, looking at the stars, I thought about the strange man that wandered into camp that evening. He didn't offer much information about himself, but he seemed to have a lot of questions for everyone else. There was more than just a little that made me wonder about him.

He never said which French company abandoned him, or the reasons why. But I guess a man was entitled to his privacy. I'd known several French traders and trappers over the years of my western expeditions. Most of them concentrated their efforts much farther north from where we were. He must have traveled a long distance before he found us. His clothes didn't look new, but they didn't show the wear they should have if he'd been in the bush for months. The men in our company wore out the clothes they started our expedition with months ago. We had all traded for leather pants, jumpers, and moccasins from friendly Indians. Clothes made from hides like elk or deer made sense out here and held up much better than what folks wear back east.

Smith offered him employment since we'd lost so many in the Indian fight. That was fine if he could earn his keep, but I had a strong feeling he was worth watching.

CHAPTER 23

The next morning when Jedediah made trapping assignments for the day, he included the new man to work with one of the veterans upstream from camp, setting traps. He didn't include me on the trapping assignment list.

"Doc," he called after giving the others their jobs for the day, "I want you to go hunting with me." It wasn't unusual for Jed and me to go hunting together. We enjoyed each other's company.

That sounded good to me. It would be one less day I'd be knee deep in cold water working traps. It might even give me an opportunity to collect some plants I hadn't seen before.

As soon as I made sure the three men left in camp with injuries had what they needed for the day, we headed into the woods. It was a damp, chilly morning with a heavy layer of fog hanging in the underbrush and ravines leading to the river.

Once we got away from the camp, we followed a game trail through the thickets expecting to spot a deer at any time. We'd survived mainly on deer and beaver meat the last few weeks. When we worked closer to the prairies, we had no trouble bagging as many antelope or buffalo as we needed. We hoped for venison that day.

Our hopes were dampened when the fog turned to light drizzle. It turned to rain about an hour and a half into our hunt.

"What do you think, Jed," I said. "Are we wasting our time today?"

"Oh, they're out there. They're just hunkered down during the rain. Maybe we ought to take their example, hang low ourselves, load fresh powder, and let the rain move through. Soon as it lets up, they'll be moving around."

Smith slid out of his pack, removed a large oilcloth we used to wrap and carry butchered meat back to camp and spread it over our heads. We sat on a log and used the trunk of a fir tree growing next to it to lean on as we prepared to remove our pan powder and replace it with fresh powder.

Jed positioned his rifle to shake the old powder from his pan when I heard a snuffling and a low, throaty growl coming from beyond where Jed sat.

Suddenly, a huge male grizzly crashed through the thicket only a few feet from us. He targeted Jed and charged straight at him. We sprang to our feet and leveled our rifles at the huge beast. Jed stood between me and the bear. I shoved my muzzle aside and removed my finger from the trigger.

The beast was five feet away when Jed thumbed the hammer back and pulled the trigger. The hammer *clicked* striking the flint. Sparks flew to the pan. No pan flash. No chamber explosion. No bullet tearing through the bear. Jed's powder was wet! The massive grizzly crushed into Jed, taking him to the ground.

I staggered back to recharge my rife. I felt helpless watching my friend's mauling. I banged my rifle stock against the tree to release the damp powder from the pan. I blew the remaining powder away as I reached to pull the plug from my powder horn. It took two tries to get the plug loose. My hands were a trembling mess. I shook too much powder on the pan. Didn't matter. Within seconds, the muzzle was again following the fight. Hammer back and finger on the trigger.

They were a blur. Jed's defense was useless. Vise-like jaws punctured and ripped his shoulder. Razor-sharp claws tore at his chest, back, shoulders, and arms. He rolled into a ball with his arms and hands covering his head for protection. Didn't work. A huge paw slung him across the ground with one swipe. Slashes ripped his head open. Part of his scalp lifted from his skull. I followed the fight through my rifle sight. No clear shot! He shoved his massive jaws around Jed's head, ready to crush his skull.

Now! I pulled the trigger. A huge billow of smoke followed the explosion. Bits of flesh and bone splattered my face. I was standing four feet away. The huge bear died instantly as the .50 caliber ball shattered his skull and tore through his brain, only inches from Jed's.

"Oh my God! Jed, are you alive?" I threw my rifle aside and dropped to my knees beside the broken man and dead bear. "Hang on, I'll get you out of there."

He was trapped under the massive bear carcass.

"Can you move your arms or legs?" I waited and listened for an answer.

"Don't know," a faint voice mumbled. "Hurts to breathe. Can't see." He struggled to get the words out."

No wonder he couldn't see. His entire face was covered in blood. I knew I'd have to get him out from under the bear so I could see the rest of his injuries. He could be bleeding to death.

Somehow, I managed to push panic aside and spoke to him. "I'll try to lift the bear's arm and head off. You push yourself out if you can." I stood over the beast and lifted.

"Now push to your left." I grimaced at the strain of lifting. He was on his belly. He managed to get his arms under him and slide his upper body from under the bear's head and arm. His hips and legs were still pinned under the heaviest part of the bear's body. I took my knife and slit what was left of his elk skin shirt up the back exposing his back and shoulders. Most of his upper body was a bloodied mess. His back, arms, hands, shoulders, and head were punctured and sliced with the bear's claws and enormous teeth. A big piece of his scalp and part of an ear was hanging loose on the side of his head.

"Do you think you're cut, or anything broken on your lower body, your legs?"

"Don't know," he managed to mumble.

"At least you can breathe now. Let me take a look and see how badly you're hurt." I didn't see any blood pumping from his body. "Hang on a minute. I need to get something to wipe the blood."

I used my knife to cut a two-foot square in the bear's skin at the shoulders. Within seconds, I'd separated the hide with the thick, cinnamon-colored hair from the body. I had a wipe.

I wiped the blood at the different puncture and cut sites. Luckily, I didn't see any damaged blood vessels. My main concern was his head wound and his difficulty breathing. I didn't know about his lower body.

"Jed, I'm going to have to pry you out from under the bear. Just relax and give me time to cut something to pry with."

I returned with a strong sapling. I shoved the pole under the bear, pushed it up, and braced it with my shoulder. That relieved enough weight off Jed's lower body so I could drag him out from under the dead bear. A quick examination told me he had no further injuries to his lower body.

"Do you think you can walk?" I asked. "We need to get you back to camp where I can sew you up."

"I don't know." His voice was a little stronger after we got the weight off him.

I managed to get him into a sitting position. His face twisted in pain as I moved him.

He held his hand lightly against his right side and tested his ribs with his fingers. "I think I have broken ribs, he said, pushing blood from his eyes with what was left of a sleeve. "Something snapped as he threw me to the ground."

I looked at him and pondered our next move. He was a pitiful sight. Blood still seeped over his face, neck, and chest from the head wound. Scalp tissue from the side of his head hung over his right eye and ear. "I don't think you can make the walk back to camp. You'll collapse before we get a hundred yards. You've lost a lot of blood. Give me a minute and I'll make a travois."

I had totally forgotten about reloading my rifle while trying to determine his condition. His weapon was totally useless as well with wet powder in the pan. I took the time necessary to reload both rifles before attempting anything else. We were lucky to be alive after the mauling. The last thing we needed while so vulnerable was to be unarmed.

I cut a few more saplings and reduced the piece of bear hide I'd used to wipe blood to strips for cordage. In a few minutes, I'd fashioned a sled type device out of sticks and poles wide and long enough for Jed to lie on while I dragged him back to camp. I blazed the trail from the bear carcass back to camp by slicing a piece of bark from a tree every couple of hundred feet. Men from the company could follow those signs to find the bear.

We were both ready for a short rest every time I cut a blaze. Riding on his belly on the travois was hard on Jed. He felt every rock, gully or small fallen log he was pulled over. The jarring caused some of his wounds to start bleeding again. I kept talking to him along the way, trying to keep him conscious. I struggled with every step, dragging him through the dense woods and briar tangles. He was a lean man, over six feet tall with a hard, working-man's body. With Jed and all of our gear tied on, there was almost two hundred and twenty pounds of dead weight on the travois.

Finally, after hours of pulling, tugging and dragging, we cleared the thicket. The sun was low in the west when I dragged Jed's travois into our camp and brought him to rest next to the fire. I dropped to my knees next to him, exhausted from the ordeal of dragging him in.

The only men in camp were the three injured we'd left that morning to continue their recovery. The others had yet to return from trapping.

"My God, who's that and what happened to him?" one of the men called out when he saw the bloody heap. Jedediah was totally unrecognizable.

"Captain Smith was attacked by a bear. He's lucky to be alive. Bring me some water and my medicine bag over there with my gear." I nodded toward my bedroll and a couple of bags next to a tree. Only one of the men could walk. He brought a bucket of water and my pack that contained a few treatment instruments, bandages, needles and thread and some medicines I'd prepared and put in vials.

"Go get more water," I said. "We're going to need lots of water.

The injured man that suddenly became my assistant was a young trapper named Garrett. He looked as scared for Jedediah as he'd been for himself when he took the arrow in his shoulder and nearly lost his hair during the Indian fight. "Is he gonna die?"

"Not if I have anything to do with it, but we've got to get him cleaned and patched up. Go on, get the water." While he was gone, I pulled a bottle whiskey from my medicine pack and started pouring it down Smith's throat. I handed the bottle to Garrett when he returned. "He'll need this," I said. "Your job is to see that he drinks as much as he can and stays comfortable."

The other men from the company started drifting into camp for the evening while I worked on Jedediah. Some hung by the fire to watch as I worked on the captain. Others went about the regular evening routine of skinning beaver, stretching hides, and tending to weapons.

I treated his head wound first while I still had good light to see. The large piece of Jed's scalp and part of his ear was attached only to a section that ran just above his eye to behind his ear.

"Jed, can you hear me," I said, after thoroughly cleaning his head and getting a fair understanding of what needed to be done.

"Yeah," he slurred and looked at me as best he could. I could see the whiskey was beginning to work.

"I've gotta do a lot of sewing on your head. Just bear with me."

"*Bear* with you?" he grinned through his pain. "Ain't I seen enough *bear* for one day?"

"Yes, I guess you have at that." I smiled at his sense of humor under the circumstances, and started the task of fitting and sewing his loose scalp and ear back onto his head.

When I was satisfied that all of Jed's injuries on his head, back, shoulders, and neck were cleaned, stitched up, and dressed, the men helped me turn him over to work on his front side. I couldn't help but notice the grimaces of a couple of veteran mountain men who'd lived through more grisly sights than they could count when they saw his face and head.

I worked on him another hour putting the pieces back together and closing the holes in his body. He would be sore for weeks. With any luck, his head had a good chance of healing satisfactorily. I'd heard of men surviving after a partial scalping by Indians with less medical care than Jed received.

After I saw he was resting comfortably for the night, I took a plate of roasted beaver one of the men handed me.

I was hungry and tired and wanted to document my day in my journal by the fire after dinner. I headed to my gear to retrieve the journal.

Where is it? Where's the waterproof bag loaded with all my research documentation and journals?

I searched the entire area within forty feet of where I slept and kept all my gear. All my other gear—my specimens, medical supplies, extra clothing and personal items were all right where they belonged. But my most important things—my journals—my reasons for being on the expedition were gone!

"Garrett!"

"Yes?" the young man answered from the other side of the camp.

I rushed, almost in a panic, to the group of men where he sat smoking his pipe.

"Garrett, were you in camp all day?"

He looked surprised at my question. He and the two other injured men were restricted to camp on my orders. "Yeah, of course. You told me to just take it easy and rest my shoulder, so that's what I did. Me, Davis and Marley were here all day."

"So, you must have some knowledge of what happened to my large, black, waterproof bag."

"You mean the one you keep all them papers in?"

"Yes, that's it. What happened to it?"

"He didn't give it to you?"

"Who?" I could feel the pounding in my head.

"Why, that feller that walked into camp last night. Claimed he was abandoned by a French trapping company. That one."

"What are you talking about?"

"He came back into camp about mid-morning, I guess. Said you'd sent him back to camp to get that big bag and bring it to you.

199

He told us you'd found something important that you wanted to document right away. We showed him where you kept your things. He opened the bag to make sure it was the one with the records you keep, threw it over his shoulder, and went back out of camp to the east. He grinned and waved at us as he headed back into the woods the way he came."

"Did he steal a horse too, or did he leave on foot?"

"He left on foot, just like he came in."

The next morning, I took four of our best trackers to follow and find the stranger that walked into our camp apparently with the purpose of stealing my documents. We were mounted and on his trail by first light.

The entire area leading in and out of our camp was awash with footprints. We'd been camped there, along the river, for almost a week, using it as a base camp. The recent rain and damp weather left mud everywhere. Men's and horse's foot and hoof prints spread out from the camp in all directions. All the prints looked similar. We all wore Indian moccasins we got in trade after our boots and shoes wore out from constant use working traps in the rivers and creeks. But the man that took my bag of documents left distinctive prints wherever he walked. He was the only man within hundreds of miles that wore leather boots with heels. He left a trail leading into the woods a blind man could follow.

"This should be easy as pie," Willis, the veteran tracker, said. He spat a stream of tobacco juice in one of the heel-shaped puddles the man in the boots left behind.

We followed his tracks onto a game trail heading east, away from camp. The heel and sole impressions continued to show their prominence on the trail for about a hundred and fifty yards. We were well out of sight of the camp when the tracker came to a stop. The rest of us drew up behind him. He rode in small circles studying the ground intently.

"What's the matter?" I asked.

"Lost the trail," he said flatly. He dismounted and let his horse's reins drag the ground. "It just stops right there." He squatted and studied the last well-defined boot print. "Y'all dismount, spread out and sweep this entire area. We'll pick 'em up somewhere around here."

We tied our horses to trees and searched the ground in all directions from the last print in the mud.

"Maybe he shed his boots and went barefoot or put on moccasins that he may have carried in his kit," one of the men hollered.

One of the other men answered, "I ain't seen no barefoot tracks and the only moccasin tracks I'm seeing are my own and yours."

We widened our search first to fifty feet beyond the last boot print. After coming up empty, we widened the search again out to a hundred feet. After two hours of intensive searching, Willis called us in for a meeting. We gathered in a small knot beside where we secured the horses.

"I'll tell you, men," Willis said shaking his head, "I ain't never seen nothin' like it. With the ground wet as it is, there should be obvious tracks on the ground. Look what we left, tryin' to pick up his tracks.

I gazed at the ground around where we stood. Everywhere you looked, marks of our moccasin prints depressed the fallen leaves and bare mud. They were so fresh; water was just beginning to seep into the depressions.

"I don't get it," I said. "It doesn't make sense. A man can't just vanish into thin air."

"I don't get it either, Doc," Willis said. "But, looks like that's exactly what happened."

A terrible, sinking feeling hit me as I stood looking at that last boot print in the mud. We had some of the best trappers *and* trackers west of the Mississippi in this company, and that man knew it. Yet he still left on foot with six months of my research just a few hours ahead of a search by experienced mounted trackers. He *knew* he wouldn't be found. *Who was that man?*

CHAPTER 24

I began to feel the separation between my spirit and my host. I knew my journey into the wilderness with Jedediah Smith and Jake McAllister was over. My aura floated from his body and hung momentarily over Jake, who never knew he'd had a visitor within, and drifted away.

I awoke well rested and refreshed and sat on the edge of my bed thinking about my latest adventure.

Wow, Jedediah Smith, the other mountain men, and early American adventurers faced the possibility of danger and death every day. I wondered if I had the courage to live the life they lived. People did what they had to do to those days to survive. Those men were tough and knew what they were getting into when they volunteered for such perilous adventures. We owe a debt of gratitude to those trailblazers who came before us and paved the way for us with their blood and sacrifice.

My curiosity about the later lives of Smith and McAllister led me to my computer to browse their names.

Jedediah Smith survived the bear attack and continued his trapping expeditions for several more years, mapping uncharted territories all the way to the Pacific Ocean and writing about his adventures. He lived a very exciting but short life. Unfortunately, he was killed by a party of Comanches as he scouted for water in present-day Kansas at only thirty-three years old.

I found mention of Doctor Jacob McAllister, a medical researcher from the nineteenth century on several online reports. It appears that his research in later life led to significant treatments for several diseases, if not cures in his time, and set the stage for future botanical research.

Grampa's magic must be really strong because he nailed it when he cautioned me to be on the lookout for strange characters that may appear not to belong at the time of my adventures. The stranger that walked into Jedediah Smith's camp and stole McAllister's bag of documentation sure met that criteria. The more I thought about it, the more alarmed I became. Grampa will want to know about that as soon as possible. That bit of intelligence was too sensitive for a phone call or email, I needed to deliver it in person.

The bike ride downtown to Grampa's place only took a little over ten minutes. Soon I stood on his porch ringing his doorbell.

"Come on in, Max," he said. "Your tone of voice on the phone sounded serious."

Breathless from the bike ride, I blurted out, "Yes, I have some important information for you."

"Come on over here to the kitchen. Catch your breath and let me get you some juice. Have you had breakfast?"

I sat on one of the stools at the kitchen bar, next to his morning paper and cup of coffee. "No, I thought what I had to tell you was more important than taking time for breakfast."

"Max, a young man needs his breakfast, regardless of the circumstances. You just relax while I get some cereal, fruit, and milk."

Soon we both sat at the bar with our bowls of cereal with strawberries. I had a glass of OJ in front of me and he had a fresh cup of coffee.

"Now," he looked at me and smiled, "tell me what has you so excited."

"You told me to be on the lookout for anybody that didn't look like they fit in while I was on my adventures."

"Yes, I remember."

I'm pretty sure I saw one of Doctor Volkov's minions, or maybe even Volkov himself while I was visiting Jake McAllister on Jedediah Smith's expedition last night."

Grampa stopped chewing and swallowed hard. His eyes turned cold. "Tell me about it."

I recounted it to him exactly as it happened. My telling of the event ended when my journey in time was over, leaving McAllister looking at the last footprint left by the stranger. "Grampa, that man just vanished into thin air."

"What did he look like?"

He was tall and slender, and here's the weird part: He only had a weeks worth of beard, and his clothes made me wonder about his story. He didn't look like he'd been in the wilderness near as long as he said."

"How tall?

"He was over six feet, maybe six-two. He was so skinny, his clothes sort of hung on him. They looked like they were too big, except his coat sleeves. They were too short. His cheeks and eyes kinda sunk into his skull. Thinking back, he was really kinda creepy looking."

"That man wasn't Doctor Volkov," Grampa said. "We've done enough research on him to know that he's only about five eight or so and his dark hair is peppered with gray. He's also of medium build, compared to your character. He has a very distinctive raised mole on his right cheek, just below the eye."

I shook my head. "No, the man I saw didn't look anything like that. What do you think all this means?"

"Obviously, Volkov has identified McAllister as a person of interest," Grampa said. "He's too greedy to just let the man do his research without interference. So, he sends one of his thugs back in time to steal his raw data. But I don't believe Volkov's organization has the advanced sophistication to interpret much of value from McAllister's raw data. What you saw was also too early in McAllister's career for him to accomplish what he did later in his lab studies."

Grampa raked his fingers through his beard. "It does concern me though that Volkov's snooping around so close to what we're researching. This isn't the first time we've found evidence of his interference with our projects. I can see that we're going to have to step up our security. Seems like Volkov is getting pretty bold, poking around to see what else he can steal. I hope Volkov's man's meddling in McAllister's affairs isn't all you experienced in your mountain man adventure."

"Oh, gosh no. I was standing four feet away from Jedediah while he was being mauled by a grizzly bear. I—well, McAllister saved Jed's life twice. First, when he shot and killed the bear that was about to eat Jed head first, and again when he got him back to camp and patched him up with a needle and thread. It was another super adventure," I grinned, "and I'm so ready for another one."

"Actually, we're working on several assignments for you that I think you'll find to be magnificent adventures, but we aren't quite ready to release them for actual time insertion. You need to enjoy your summer a little. This is the Fourth of July week. I want you to take a few days and enjoy the holiday. Go have some fun with your friends. We should have something I think you'll really enjoy next week."

That night I shared the whole Jedediah Smith adventure with Mom, Dad, and Megan. It felt really good being able to share my wild adventures with the family.

CHAPTER 25

Grampa was right. That was a big holiday week and our town gets really wound up about the Fourth of July. Some of the old-timers around town say we don't need much of an excuse to have a party. People decorate their homes and property with American flags and bunting, especially in the historical district. There's always a big patriotic parade that loops around downtown, and a fun festival with lots of merchandise and food vendors on the parking lots on the courthouse square. The sandy beach at the lake, right off the main drag going toward downtown is crowded and there's always a rodeo too. People come from all over and jam the square for the parade and festival and hang around to visit the shops and restaurants. There are bands and music all day with pie eating contests and fireworks after dark. It's always a fun place to be. Every year, we're right in the middle of it.

Mom, Dad, Megan and I met Grampa at his house and walked the short distance downtown to the square for the parade and festival. We arrived about an hour before the parade. The sidewalks around the courthouse square where the vendors set up were overflowing with people. Dad said that people come from all over north and central Texas for our Independence Day celebration.

Megan found several girlfriends on the sidewalk as we turned the corner onto the town square, so she joined them. "I'll see y'all at our regular spot to watch the parade," she called over her shoulder as she went with her friends to see if the festival vendors offered anything they hadn't seen before. I also ran into Rick and Jeremy in the crowd and spun off from Mom, Dad, and Grampa to hang out with them before the parade.

Our families always came together in time to see the beginning of the parade. We took turns with Rick' and Jeremy's families and a couple of Megan's friend's families to reserve a spot at the beginning of the parade route for all of us. It's like a huge party when we all got together under our sun-shade canopies to watch the parade.

I was walking with the guys following the flow of the crowd, checking the vendor's booths and people watching, mainly girl watching, taking an occasional snapshot with my cell phone's camera when something else caught my eye.

A guy was walking toward us. He was about sixty yards away. I could tell, even at that distance, there was something peculiar about him. *What was it?* He was tall, over six-feet. He was middle-aged, clean-shaven, and so thin his cheeks and dark eyes were sunken into his skull. For some reason, he just didn't seem to blend in with the people having a good time in the crowd. He wasn't looking at any of the booths or the merchandise in them. He was looking at people's faces. In his hand was a piece of paper that he looked at occasionally, then returned to studying people's faces as they approached. Out of curiosity while he was still a good distance away, I pointed and shot a photo. For some reason, I seemed to be drawn to him. *Why?*

As he got closer, I took another shot. He totally ignored me. He was looking at an old man holding a little girl's hand. The old man and little girl seemed to be following the rest of her family. Mister Tall and Skinny was focusing on older men. By then, he was only a few feet from me and looking at a different older man. I took two photos. The second shot moved downward, off target when Rick nudged me on the shoulder. "Hey man," he said, "quit goofing off with your phone. Let's go. There's lots more to see and the parade's starting soon."

"You guys go ahead," I said, turning and looking at the back of the tall man walking away. "I'll catch up with you in a minute." I was still baffled as to why that guy caught and held my attention.

I walked behind one of the vendor booths onto the thick grass and shade under one of the giant pecan trees next to the courthouse. I needed the shade to get a better view of the photos I'd just taken.

I switched my phone from camera to gallery mode and sat on the grass. The first two distance photos were just that—a crowd with a tall guy in the distance. I couldn't tell much about him.

When I clicked on the next photo, the closeup, it hit me like a ton of bricks. The skinny face I was looking at belonged to the same man that stole Jake McAllister's bag of documents from Jedediah Smith's camp—one-hundred-and-ninety years ago! I was certain. Even though he was clean shaven, there was no mistaking that face.

There was one more photo in the sequence. My finger hovered over the small image, expecting it to be blurred because my shot was pulled downward by Rick. I clicked on it. A perfectly clear image of a face filled the entire screen.

Oh No!

Rick's interference with my camera aim caused my hand to move down just enough to get a clear image of the skinny man's hand holding an 8 ½ x 11 photo of my grandfather's face. *He's looking for Grampa!*

I had to get to Grampa. Fast. He and the family were on the far side of the square and down the main street a few blocks toward the beginning of the parade. I knew the crowd would slow me down. I had to get away from the crowd *and* the bad guy.

I shot across the grass and into the side door of the old stone courthouse in the middle of the square. It had a wide hallway that ran the length of the building from one side to the other. I dashed through the historic building, dodging a few festival organizers along the way.

I ignored a lady yelling, "hey, slow down there!" as I whizzed by her table set up in the hallway. I blasted through the wide door at the far end of the building, back into the sunlight, and down the steps. I had to brave the festival crowd again as I ran across the parking lot and into the street that had been cleared with barricades for the parade.

I could hear the high school band and see the flashing lights of the police cars at the beginning of the parade coming my way. The parade had started seven blocks away, but the street was clear between me and my family. I made that empty street my own as I sprinted the four blocks to where the family waited. Parade officials yelled at me to clear the street, but nobody took chase after me. Within seconds I reached my family along with the group of friends under one of the many sun canopies along the parade route.

"Where's the fire?" Dad said laughing. "Never seen you so anxious to watch the parade."

"Dad, Grampa, come back here with me. I need to tell you something." Dad's expression changed when he saw the anxiety on my face. I grabbed him by the shirt sleeve, and lead him behind the people crowded along the sidewalk. Grampa followed.

Once out of earshot of the others, I said, "Look here." I tried to slow my breathing to catch my breath as I called up the photo gallery on my phone. I found the close-up of the skinny guy on my phone and pointed to the photo. "That's the guy I was telling you about from my last adventure. He's the one that stole all of Doctor McAllister's documents. I'm sure of it. He's right here in town today. He's looking for you, Grampa. Look at this." I clicked on the next photo showing Grampa's face. "That's what he's carrying. He's going through the crowd trying to find you."

Grampa's face took on a look I hadn't seen before. He was no longer the grampa out for a fun day with his family. He suddenly became a warrior king, ready to defend his castle.

"Tom, tell Susan and Megan to meet us later at the house. They're under no threat of harm. I need you and Max to come with me. We must go now."

While Dad told Megan and Mom to enjoy the parade and festival, and we'd see them later at Grampa's house, Grampa reached in his pocket and pulled out a communication device. It wasn't a phone. It looked like the walkie-talkie Hatch used the time we were in the garden to call Grampa in his shop to let him know I was visiting.

"Control, this is Command One," Grampa said into the device with a voice of authority. "Implement security level orange immediately. Repeat, implement security level orange immediately. Understand?" He hesitated a moment, listening. "Prepare for my arrival at access location delta with two passengers."

While on his communication device, his eyes scanned the area.

"This way," he said as Dad joined us after making arrangements to meet later with Mom and Megan. Grampa led us across the parking lot of a government building to a metal-walled alcove at the side of the building where they kept the dumpster out of sight.

Once inside the enclosure, he stepped between Dad and me and reached into his pocket to pull out two little strips of leather. They were bookmarks like I had in my big book. After rolling them into tight tubes, he held one in each hand and reached his arms around Dad's and my shoulders, pulling us close. "Put your arms around my waist and hold on," he said and squeezed the leathers.

CHAPTER 26

A huge blast of wind enveloped us. Suddenly, Dad, Grampa, and I found ourselves standing inside a screen of bushes in the back corner of Grampa's garden. We were six—no—seven blocks away from the dumpster alcove. Grampa released his grasp from us, looked at a camera partially hidden in a tree overhead, and waved.

A six-foot-wide portion of the flower bed right next to us—dirt, mulch, plants—all of it, started moving. The whole planting bed was housed in a huge metal container. It lifted silently and stopped five feet off the ground. It was supported by some sort of heavy hydraulic arms. Underneath was a lighted concrete stairway leading to a tunnel.

Looking into the tunnel, Dad said, "What the—"

"Hold on," Grampa said. "I know this is a lot to take in. I'll explain everything soon. Just follow me."

When we cleared the entrance to the tunnel, the mechanical lift that elevated the large planter bed closed and sealed behind us. The stairway took us into a concrete-walled tunnel. We followed it to a security door. After Grampa went through his access procedures, the lock clicked and we pushed through. We walked into the middle of the exercise equipment in the recreation lounge of Grampa's bunker.

Grampa turned to face us. "Sorry for the high drama," he said, "but I was a little busy and really had no time to explain things to you.

"With what Max showed us, I had to return home as rapidly as possible without going through downtown and face the possibility of being detected by Volkov's man, so I used my point-to-point transport system. I'll explain all that later. I needed you two to come with me because you both need to know our security capability. We'll fill Susan and Megan in later."

"Wait a minute," Dad said. His hair was disheveled from the blast of wind. He wore a look of stupefaction. "What just happened is impossible. One moment we're standing next to a dumpster and then all of a sudden, poof," he flung his arms into the air, "we're halfway across town standing inside a bunch of bushes in your garden. It's impossible, but it just happened!"

"Yes," Grampa said calmly. "Amazing, isn't it." I use a combination of a physical dimension warp and a very powerful channel of magic to accomplish it. You can imagine the number of bumps and bruises I got perfecting it. It comes in handy sometimes, though."

Dad still looked perplexed. "But I was with you. I have no power."

"You were simply a passenger. Kind of like cargo. I carried you along using my transport power.

"Now, let me show you why I brought you with me. You'll need to know all about this sooner or later. It might as well be sooner."

He walked across the room to the counter by the door and looked at the rear wall with the artwork of athletes in motion. He reached under the countertop and pressed a hidden button.

All the large art panels ascended into the ceiling as if they were sucked up by a vacuum. Bright lights illuminated the area behind the disappearing wall, revealing an additional secret room. It was a warehouse loaded for action. The left side of the room was devoted to weaponry.

The wall and two shelving units were full of every modern police and paramilitary weapons and devices one could imagine, both lethal and non-lethal. Tasers, rubber bullet launchers, semi-automatic handguns, long guns, and rocket-propelled grenade launchers covered the wall—floor to ceiling and filled up the two shelves. Cases of hand-grenades were stacked on the floor. Shelves were stacked high with fully loaded ammo clips. Even a small track driven armored robot waited in a corner, ready to be called into action.

Most of the back wall of the room was made of heavy glass with a steel door in the middle. It took me a moment to realize that beyond the glass was a soundproof shooting range. The tunnel we traveled on the way to the recreation lounge apparently ran alongside the underground range.

The right side of the room was a locker area dedicated to storing combat uniforms and personal paramilitary accessories. Armored vests, gas masks, and helmets hung from racks on the wall along with every other piece of military apparel and accessories imaginable. Hatch, Rocky, and Kat were there; already in their camo t-shirts, cargo pants, and boots, and were finishing strapping protective vests and other gear on their bodies.

I turned, mouth agape to look at Grampa. "What in the world?"

"We're prepared to do whatever it takes to protect the House of Discovery. We all, including myself, wear many different hats, including this one." He reached to a shelf and pitched military helmets to me and Dad. He took one for himself, nodding for us to follow his example by strapping it on.

Next he handed us body armor vests. He continued explaining as we strapped those on. "Everybody here except Jeffery and I have strong military backgrounds. But don't sell us short because of our lack of *formal* military training. We've probably received better training right here in advanced security and weapons training than most military specialists anywhere."

He led us across the room to the weapons section where he selected a semi-automatic .45 caliber hand gun, four clips of ammo and a webbed utility belt. After fitting the belt around his waist, he shoved a clip into the weapon, loaded a round in its chamber, set the safety and holstered it. Then he loaded the remaining ammo in their pouches on his belt, and turned to face us.

"You see, in his career, Hatch here," he nodded toward Hatch, "trained the best military snipers in the world. He's also a master of hand-to-hand combat.

"Rocky's been called upon time and time again to teach advanced security measures at the Navy War College in Monterey,

California to mid-grade officers who will one day become Navy admirals and Marine generals.

"Between the two of them, they've given Jeffery everything he needs to meet the protection and security needs of the team. And Kat has given us all a good working over in the process of teaching us personal defense through martial arts. Even I feel comfortable defending myself, my team and The House as necessary."

He turned to his team and verified they were outfitted to engage whatever comes their way. Finding them ready, he said, "all right, we'll continue Condition Orange for at least the next twenty-four hours." He nodded toward me, "Max has a photo on his phone of a person of interest. He's downtown right now. Max, I need to ask you to send Kat a copy of that image." He turned to Hatch. "Hatch, deploy the long-range photo drones to search the crowd downtown until you find that individual and put him on surveillance until further notice.

"That guy in town looking for me constituted a threat. I don't know what he's doing here, how he knew to look for me here, or how long he'll be here. We'll find all that out soon enough, but I put The House under high alert just in case." He nodded to the others gearing up in the arsenal. "We don't expect trouble, but we're ready.

He turned to Dad and me. "I want to make one thing very clear to you two. And I'll say this here in front of the rest of the team. Participation in the defense of The House is not a requirement of the job here." He turned to those gearing up. "Right guys?"

"That's right," Hatch said, snugging a utility belt loaded with ammo clips around his waist, "but we all volunteer to be a part of it. We know better than anybody just how important it is to protect what's in that vault. Besides," he grinned, "it keeps us well trained and on our toes. We may not be chasing bad guys around the desert or mountains, or through a bombed out town halfway around the world like we used to, but the adrenalin rush is the same."

Grampa nodded his agreement and turned to Dad and me. "Now, let's talk about you two. Tom, one of the factors that made you attractive to us is your military record. Yes, we accessed your records.

"Max, did you know your father's a decorated war hero?"

"Who? Him?" I looked surprised. "I knew he was in a war in the Middle East and had some medals he kept in a drawer, but he never talked about it. Wow, a war hero?"

"That was a long time ago." Dad looked embarrassed. "And I wasn't any hero. Just did my job."

"His medals prove otherwise," Grampa said.

Dad grinned. "You guys sure know how to make a man feel welcome. With my family's approval, I'm in, but what about Max, his sister, and mom? They're all a part of The House of Discovery now, but certainly not ready for what these guys are prepared for."

I looked at Dad and Grampa. "Yeah, where do I fit in?"

"I'm glad you asked that," Grampa said, looking at me. He had that same old twinkle in his eye. "I think I have a perfect plan for you—Megan too, and your mom, if she wishes.

Max, if you're willing, and your mom and dad agree, we'll start you on a training program to get you involved in some research projects. You can also start monitoring security and reporting future threats." He grinned. "Looks like you've already started that by finding that character in town.

"You can work in the control center a few hours a week, as long as it doesn't interfere with school or your social life which are both very important to a young man your age.

"Then, later as you mature and are ready for more hands-on security activity, we'll get you involved in more of whatever you and your parents agree. Obviously, it can't have anything to do with weapons until you're at least of legal age. Then we'll all be a part of that decision. In the meantime, if you want to be their student, Kat and Hatch can become your mentors in hand to hand martial arts.

"But the most exciting things you'll be doing the rest of your life will be your magnificent adventures in time.

"Along with more American explorations, there are so many exciting incidents all over the world that need your attention. You can discover lost and forgotten documents and treasure from the middle ages in Europe to the ancient cultures of Asia and the Andes. You can travel through time to visit the cradle of civilization in the Middle East and see what space looks like from the eyes of an American astronaut.

"It's also time for you to start learning more about the details of the magic you possess, and how to use it. It took me a lifetime of trial and error to finally understand and develop the powers I manage now. You have those same powers, and much more than I was ever able to tap. They just need to be awakened. With the technology available at your fingertips and the recent advancements in science, there's no limit to what you'll be able to achieve; far beyond my clumsy accomplishments.

"It's also apparent from what we saw today, our enemies are rearing their ugly heads. We cannot let them crack our defenses. We must be ready to preserve the secrets of the House of Discovery and the future of the world it holds.

"So, Max, are you ready for the most extraordinary adventures of your life?"

I looked at him with the biggest grin I'd ever worn. "Captain Discovery is more than ready. Beam me up, Grampa, let's do this!"

The End

About the Author

Dan Vanderburg, a sixth generation Texan, always enjoyed history. Proud of his heritage, he researched his ancestors and other pioneers to learn of their exciting lives on the American frontier. The more he researched, the more he developed a desire to write about those extraordinary people that made America what it is. He started writing in 1995 with a few scribbled notes that ultimately led to publishing his first novel, *Legacy of Dreams*. Additional novels, short stories and poetry followed.

Dan is a member of The Sons of The Republic of Texas, serves as a docent at the Bridge Street History Museum in Granbury, Texas and serves on the Hood County, Texas Historical Commission. He lives and writes in Granbury, Texas. In 2019 Granbury was voted the Best Historical Small Town in America. Learn more about Dan at: DanVanderburg.com.

More Books by Dan Vanderburg Available at Amazon.com:

Legacy of Dreams (Texas Legacy Family Saga Book 1)

Trail of Hope (Texas Legacy Family Saga Book 2)

Freedom Road (Texas Legacy Family Saga Book 3)

The Littlest Hero

The Extraordinary Adventures of Max Malone (Volume 1, Tales of Texas)

Happy Sounds (A Collection of Humorous Short Stories and Captivating Poetry)

Strange and Sweet (Stories from the Granbury Writers' Bloc—Dan Contributed 3 Short Stories and 3 Poems to the Collection)

DAN VANDERBURG

Made in the USA
Monee, IL
18 January 2021

56244343R00132